Marietta
and the Creeping Nasties

by Shannon Perry

The Charles E. Walters Company
New York, New York

First printing 2002

ISBN 0-9723902-0-0

LCCN 2002094554

Acknowledgments

From the author:

> To my parents, George and Prudence Perry, for a childhood so storybook fun and mud-wonderful, I may never leave it.

> With great, sticky piles of thanks to Bill Walters, for the only nickname I ever liked and for pushing me into publication; to Nikki McNurlen, best-ever cheerleader, right down to the metaphorical pom poms, and to Jakub Fiala, true Bohemian, for lightness of heart.

From the illustrator:

Thanks to painters Gary Fagin, Charles Emerson and Michael Stasinos who have been so generous with their training and feedback. Special thanks to John Keenan, Mary Jo and Glenn Dalrymple, Brett and Barbara Lither, Renee and Robert Kleemann, Jim and Joanna McCormick, Stephanie and Aileen Raymond, Robert Reeder, Dana Doerkerson, Libya Vogt, Emma Vokurka, Daved Farrell, and William Meyer.

Character List (in order of appearance):

Marietta: A girl from Earth, hero of Incunabula, friend of the dragons, accomplished swordfighter and all-around good person to have on your side.

Marietta's Mom: Would probably rather not know how much danger Marietta encountered in Incunabula.

Bumble: A puppy we never meet but who plays a rather important role anyway.

the Tumble-Down Wizard: A very clumsy fellow who falls down a lot but is clever enough to recognize Marietta's talents. Also clever enough to fit in a costume the size of a cat. But he won't tell how he does it, so don't even bother to ask.

the Rainbow Maker: Where did you think rainbows came from? Grumpy but kind.

the Queen of Quiet Mountain: She's a queen. She lives on Quiet Mountain. Well, if you knew that already, why did you ask?

Shadowlark: The most troublesome but also the best and truest of friends. He's a bird who's constantly in need of saving, but in the end, it may be Shadowlark who saves us all.

the Moon-Shadow Tigers: Giant tigers the size of elephants, they ride on moonbeams. They are the guardians of Incunabula and not to be messed with.

Promises-Kept Clerk: A dullard. What a terribly terribly awfully dull person. A snooze. Avoid at parties.

the Dark Prince of Dullardry: The bad guy, evil through and through. He wants to destroy Incunabula and all its magic and wonder.

Perfectly Frank: The biggest liar in all of Incunabula, he always sticks a finger in his left ear when he lies. A terribly silly person, really.

the Boatkeeper and Nellie: Once a mounted lamp-keeper and his flying horse, they're now a boatkeeper and a boat, thanks to a spell from a grumpy, ill-tempered witch.

the Storyteller: He lives in the Apex Pagoda and collects all the stories ever told. He may have some answers about the origin of the Dark Prince. And how to defeat him . . .

Fester and Ooze: the twin heads of the Ravenous Dragon of Gibbet Hill. Bad breath, bad temper, bad attitude times two.

the Illuminated Lady: person of importance in the Illuminated Village, she is in charge of the Village Prism.

Mistress of Tides: A grumpy, ill-tempered witch, she's invisible now and not happy about it. Controls water -- rivers, oceans, etc.

Max-he's-such-a-*good*-boy: A boy from Earth, he's pretty much worn out his welcome in Incunabula . . .

Assorted trolls, elves, magical creatures and an albatross.

Chapter One

The question of what to do with a rainy Sunday is at least as old as Sundays and possibly as old as rain. Marietta sat staring out her window, trying hard not to think about her bicycle or her baseball mitt or the fact that on a *normal* Sunday, she'd be riding one and carrying the other to the park for a game that would last all afternoon. But the rain was coming down hard enough to leave little holes in the dirt of the flower bed, and even Marietta's parents – who were normally quite reasonable about things like rain and mud and riding a bicycle no-handed – wouldn't let her out in rain that could leave dents in her head.

She'd already played Monopoly with the cat (and won, as she almost always did), she'd gotten the mud off her soccer cleats, she'd cleaned her bicycle and spoken soothingly to it (thunder made it skittish). She'd held her puppy, Bumble, until a crash of thunder had sent him scampering, tail between his legs, into the closet to hide from the monster. There simply wasn't anything else to do but stare out the window and sigh. And just sighing seemed like such a waste of her precious remaining weekend hours.

It really didn't help that she'd seen Billy-down-the-block take off down the street on his new birthday bike. Rain or no rain, dented head notwithstanding, Billy got to do whatever he wanted, and was King of his own Sunday Afternoons while Marietta was a prisoner of Rain.

That funny cat was on the fence again. He was sitting quite contentedly under the fat old oak tree whose branches grew so thick and heavy that little rain got through. He was staring at her again, so Marietta stared back. That occupied her for awhile.

"Marietta!"

"In here, Mom."

"What are you up to, sweetie?" Her mother poked her blonde head into Marietta's blue bedroom. "Daydreaming again?"

"That cat's here again. I'm watching him. Something's very strange about that animal. He just doesn't behave like cats are supposed to."

"So it's not a cat? Funny, it looks just like one."

"I know it *looks* like one, but it doesn't act like one. Last night it sang that aria that dad likes. From Puccini. I'm sure of it."

Marietta's mother laughed and sat next to her on the bed. "Cats rarely sing arias, in *my* experience, but that may be because I hang out with the wrong kinds of cats. Speaking of animals, where's Bumble?"

Marietta pointed to her closet. The door was nearly closed, but her mother could just see the tip of a quivering tail. "He doesn't like the thunder, so he stuck his head in the dirty laundry. He thinks if he can't see the monster, the monster can't see him."

"Poor little guy. Oh, Marietta, Mrs. Franzen called. She says thank you again for baby-sitting last night, but would you please not tell little Jenny that her umbrella is really a bat that will fly away with her the next time it's opened? They nearly missed church this morning because Jenny refused to come out from under her bed."

Marietta smiled, a little sheepishly. "Sorry. She takes everything so seriously."

"And remember when Charlie wouldn't sleep for weeks because he wanted to see his pillows dance at midnight? How are you going to pay for your college education with baby-sitting money if no one will ask you to baby-sit?"

"The little kids love my stories."

"But their parents aren't so thrilled. Speaking of college educations, you might consider doing your homework, if you're really terribly bored."

"I did *consider* it, actually."

"You might do more than just consider it, then. How about that?"

"I think the rain is slowing down," said Marietta, though she really didn't, and just as she spoke the words, a loud crash of thunder startled the funny cat, and it toppled off the fence and out of sight. "Uh oh. I'd better go make sure that cat's all right."

"The cat is fine, Marietta. The fence is barely three feet high. Crack a book, and you'll see how quickly the afternoon will pass. Geography, perhaps?" Her mother rumpled her hair fondly, then left, quietly shutting the door behind her.

Marietta dragged her geography book out from under her other school books and opened it. Geography was Marietta's worst subject. Maps made her impatient – just seeing all those exotic names made her so desperate to get out and see the real thing. Paper mountains and rivers made of squiggly blue lines and forests that were nothing more than great green swathes of ink on paper: these were no more real life than Sunday cartoons were real people.

Billy likes geography, Marietta thought. *Billy gets As on every test, he can find every stupid, wandering river, every fat, clumsy mountain, every heaving, burping volcano-* Enough! Marietta slammed the book shut and stared fiercely out the window again.

The cat, now thoroughly soaked and bedraggled and cross, staggered back up the fence and plumped down under the oak tree. The cat had been visiting Marietta every day for nearly a week now, and Marietta had left food and water out for it and wondered where it lived and why it chose their yard to hang out in. It was an odd animal and did things that weren't quite cat-like. Marietta decided it would be sort of like a science project if she were to sit in this window and study that cat. She made herself comfortable, there in her rainy window, and prepared for a long afternoon.

Chapter Two

Just on the other side of Marietta's world, just left of the mirror that sat on her dresser, was an entirely different place that Marietta had no idea existed. It's called the Land of Incunabula. You've never heard of it, have you? In fact, most Earth people have never heard of it, though it has been Earth's nearest neighbor since the beginning. Scientists frequently overlooked it, looking just over the top of it, around it, even *through* it without seeing it at all. And it's too bad, really, as knowing of the existence of Incunabula would answer a lot of Earth's oddest questions.

Now, I know that it's difficult to believe in things like other worlds that exist on the far side of the looking glass, and you must pick and choose what you will believe and how you will believe it. Personally, I find I believe best on Tuesdays, early in the morning. I can believe nearly *anything* on a Tuesday morning. But I'm quite skeptical on Wednesdays and Saturdays and find it very difficult to believe even the least impossible of impossible things. I suppose you have no idea where Tuesdays and Wednesdays and Saturdays come from, do you? Make yourself comfortable, and I'll explain.

Back in the time when the Land of Incunabula (that's Ink-yoo-**nab**-yoo-luh) was so new that God still had to consult the Owner's Manual from time to time, the days of the week were all one day, all joined together into one generous clump of time. And when the days of the week are all joined together, then there's plenty of time for all the things you need to do: time for strawberry picking and dandelion blowing, time for puddle-splashing and puppy hugging and leaf-pile jumping. It was a lovely system when no one could tell the days of work from the days of play so people worked when work was required and played when it wasn't.

But along came crotchety old Duty on his crooked stick and ripped Monday from the pile, leaving a great hole in the week and Sunday evening stained with Monday's blood. Then came Ambition in a sharp Italian suit and alligator shoes and took Tuesday, who wriggled in the grip of Ambition but could not get free. Directly behind him was Competition who thought Wednesday would be the best day to have and grabbed him before anyone else could get their hands on him. Necessity, having birthed Invention, stole Thursday to feed her hungry child, and finally, Guilt slithered in and pilfered Friday, although a bit of Friday got snagged on Saturday's button and remained behind. Saturday and Sunday were frightened and clung together, but eventually Indulgence and Piety would stake claims on them, and though the two days could never be divided entirely, their hold on one another would never be the same. These, then, became the seven separate days, torn from their happy union to lead seven separate lives, and those who had split them apart laughed at them and called them weak — which is why we call them a "week" to this day.

For a very long while, that was all that happened, and the Incunabulans adapted. But after that very long while was over, other changes began slowly taking place as well: sunny days started disappearing and being replaced with drippy wet days. Books full of stories about adventures and dragons slowly, one-by-one, became textbooks about mathematics and charts about the evaporation rates of earthworm sweat and centipede spit, and who would want to read about that? Lovely questions like *how are you* and *isn't it a wonderful day today* and *would you like a piece of chocolate?* were drying up in people's mouths, so when they tried to ask a question all that came out was a puff of dust and questions like *why are you such a horrible child* and *have you eaten all your asparagus* and *what in heaven's name is a unicorn?* And it got worse. Smiles were vanishing at a rate of 1500 per minute, and all the flowers turned to poison ivy, and the cherries never got ripe but instead turned black and rotten before dropping with a wet, smelly *plop* from the tree. But the very last straw of all was when the candies, the lovely chocolates and the hard sweets that you can suck on for an afternoon, all the chewy fruity stickies and the crunchy toffee crumbles turned all at once and with no warning into *black licorice*. Now really, that was simply going too far.

The scientists bleached and ironed their white coats and stuck pencils and pens behind their ears and calculators and measuring tapes into their pockets and started to research these horrible happenings. They poked and prodded and listened and measured and scribbled and questioned and consulted and argued and did all those things that scientists do. They got together in little groups and wrote reports on this research, and the little groups formed bigger groups and they read their reports and agreed that they were certainly very fine reports, and then they went on television and said that they had collected some very fine reports and were well satisfied with their work.

In the end, they offered this diagnosis: the world of Incunabula was currently suffering from a condition known in scientific circles as the "Creeping Nasties." And then the scientists went away again, back into their laboratories and libraries, not to be seen again until the next national emergency.

Now, a diagnosis is a very helpful thing, particularly when one knows the cure. But this was a very different case: no one had ever heard of the Creeping Nasties, and no one knew what the cure was or how to stop it from spreading. Some even speculated that it wasn't a real disease, just something the scientists had come up with because they couldn't think of anything else, but those people weren't much listened to.

Meanwhile, the lemonade had turned to cough syrup and the ice cream had turned to snow with some very suspicious patches of yellow. Things were getting worse, and no one knew what to do.

A very large Citizens' Council meeting was called, and many suggestions were offered. Someone said a universal dose of cod-liver oil was just the thing to set their world to rights, but someone else pointed out that this had already happened when all the maple syrup turned to cod-liver oil overnight, and that hadn't solved the problem, had it? Another person said that three days of continuous singing and dancing would be very pleasant and would drive the Creeping Nasties away, but the musicians objected, since all the music they played these days came out as funeral dirges, and the singers agreed, because their very fine voices now sounded like a chorus of bullfrogs. The citizens were growing desperate: colors were fading before their eyes, and the tribes that lived in the Snowlands said all their snowmen were skinny and vicious and gave the children nightmares. Finally, a small, quiet voice spoke up from the back of the room.

"I think I know what's wrong."

Everyone in the room gasped, and those in the back immediately began pushing the speaker forward, to the front where everyone could hear him. They pushed him right the way through the crowd and up onto the platform where the most important citizens stood, and right in front of the amplifying monkey so his voice could be heard.

"I think I know what's happening to Incunabula," he said quietly, and the amplifying monkey screeched his words to the crowd. "The children of Earth are losing interest in us; they don't believe in us anymore, and so the Creeping Nasties have come. It's our own fault, really: when was the last time we sent a legion of fairies to play at the bottom of someone's garden? How many unicorns have been dispatched to Earth in the past five hundred years? When was the last time we hosted a changeling child stolen from a human crib and replaced by one of our own magic children? Our Interplanetary Exchange Program hasn't swapped a single infant in the dark of night in centuries. How can we expect them to believe in us if we don't sometimes remind them that we're here?"

The people of Incunabula were rather insulted. They didn't like being reprimanded for bad behavior from a tumble-down wizard like this one. For the wizard wasn't a very impressive wizard at all. He was rather raggedy and flopsy and all-thrown-together, and he made you think that perhaps his head was on his shoulders today only because that was where it had landed when he threw it, and maybe on other days he wore it on one elbow or stuck to his knee. On his head, perched like a nervous bird, was a conical hat covered in stars and planets. A long robe swished around his feet, and a beard clutched at the end of his chin and stumbled and staggered down his chest and belly like a clumsy, aging ferret before coming to an abrupt end somewhere around his knees. He was a tangled, rambling sort of a wizard with little glasses that perched on an inquisitive nose and pockets stuffed with paper and pencils and unidentifiable little bits of pieces of fragments of something-or-other that really weren't terribly important.

The bespectacled, tumble-down wizard was in charge of writing everything down. That was his job. He stood in corners or perched on the furniture, or, if the day was bad enough, hid under the table, scribbling notes and chewing the end of his pencil. He had begun by documenting all the types of love that exist in the world (eleven thousand, nine hundred and forty-nine, to be exact) — everything from love for the way puppies always want to lick your ears (#17), to love for the way sunlight slants in a winter window (#8,146); from love that hits you from behind (#942), to love that was there all along but hidden under a blanket in an old, musty trunk in the back of the attic and discovered just in the nick of time (#11,807) — but when that task was concluded, he found he simply wanted to go on, watching the world and the creatures in it, taking his notes and disturbing the peace only with the quiet scratching of pen on paper.

He knew lots and lots of things, as one will if one watches and listens closely enough and for long enough. He knew all about the patterns of spots on a ladybug's back (did you know that no two ladybugs ever wear the same dots? They don't, especially not to fancy balls or dinner parties), and he could identify the nine kinds of giggles of a happy baby and the best way to stack scoops of ice cream so they don't fall no matter how tall the tower is. He had notes on every person in Incunabula, and while this certainly made him very knowledgeable, it didn't make him very popular. He was generally regarded as a bit nosy and rather too curious, but he was a very gentle wizard who never used what he knew to hurt other people, so they let him scribble in his notebooks and didn't bother him too much. But they did know to listen to him now, even if they didn't much like what he had to say.

"What should we do?" cried the Emperor of Cheese. "The cheese my cows are producing is so hot you'd think I fed them nothing but jalapeno peppers and mustard seeds! No one can eat so much as a bite of my splendid cheeses, and my cows are growing thin from sadness!"

"Oh, yes!" cried the Duke and Duchess of Popcorn, leaping from their chairs for the eighty-ninth time that evening for they found it terribly difficult to keep still, "our popcorn hardly ever pops, and when it does, it gives off a terrible smell. Instead of white, fluffy clouds, our popcorn is gray and wet and squishy. We haven't heard a lovely *crunch!* in weeks!"

Suddenly the meeting became a horrible jumble of shouting and confusion. Everyone had a Creeping Nasty story to tell; flowers grew upside-down this year so all you could see were the roots, and the bumblebees had stopped making honey and started making liver-and-onions instead, and the street signs now pointed only to the most unpleasant places, and in some places, where the Creeping Nasties had spread furthest and quickest, if you tried to smile, your lips would crack as they usually did only on the coldest of winter days. Oh, the situation was desperate indeed, but the tumble-down wizard just stood calmly on the platform and listened and didn't try to shout above the crowd. Finally, the yelling died down, and everyone went back to their chairs.

They sat and looked up at the wizard, waiting to hear what medicine would cure ailing Incunabula.

"We need a child from Earth," said the wizard, when the room was still and quiet, "An Earth child who is special and extraordinary and who will have great adventures here and take them back to Earth and tell them to all the other children who will start to believe in us again."

"We don't have time for a changeling child!" cried Uncle Time (brother of our Father Time here on Earth), consulting one of the many watches that dangled from his clothes and filled his pockets. "An infant takes many years to raise, and the Creeping Nasties are moving too fast. Just look!" he shouted, waving one of his watches at the crowd, "Nearly half of my watches now run backwards, and some of them don't run at all, and four of my best watches have run away completely. How can I keep Time like this? If any more of my watches stop working, I shall have to keep Time in a box beneath my bed!"

Panic threatened to disrupt the meeting a second time, but the wizard just nodded solemnly at Uncle Time, and he seemed so calm and unconcerned that the rest of the Incunabulans quickly grew quiet again.

"I don't mean a changeling child, Uncle Time, for you're quite right that we don't have enough time for one. I suggest that instead, I go to Earth and select a child for the job."

"Will it work?" asked the Princess of Chocolate, in her sweet, rich, brown voice. "Will we be able to convince the children of Earth? They've gone beyond us," she sighed, "and I wonder if we'll be able to get them back."

"Yes," said the Incunabulans to one another, "*can* the children of Earth still believe? Will they remember that Halloween has more to do with ghosts and witches than with candy corn and caramel apples? Do they think there's a goblin in the wardrobe or just clothes and shoes? What do they see when they look under the bed? Trolls or dustballs? Perhaps the children of Earth have forgotten how to *believe*?"

And one rather famous fairy, who was still weak because not enough children had clapped, tinkled her sad agreement as the sunlight grew dimmer and dimmer.

The wizard spent many weeks on Earth, wandering about, trying to find that most extraordinary child who would save Incunabula from the Creeping Nasties. But so many Earth children were dullards, the wizard began to wonder if there was some connection: when children stopped believing in places like Incunabula or in creatures like the Chestnut Trolls who lived in trees and threw nuts down on the heads of people passing below, or the Shadow Sweepers whose job it was to sweep out the last of the night shadows when morning came, did they then turn into dullards? And these dullards, these legions of empty-eyed, empty-headed, shallow-hearted children, were they the cause of the Creeping Nasties? It made the wizard shudder to think so, for there were so *many* dull children here on Earth, so many who found it unthinkable to pick up a book or impossible to find animal shapes amongst the clouds without a diagram and instructions.

But still the wizard couldn't give up hope; he had to find an Earth child who could help save his homeland. So he went on, wearing all kinds of different disguises, waiting to see that spark in a child's eyes that indicated an adventurer, a dreamer, a brave, courageous and kind child who would have adventures that dull children couldn't even dream of. But *where* was that very special child?

And that had led him here, to the fence outside Marietta's window, on that wretched, rainy Sunday that would change both their lives forever.

Marietta had known from the very first night that the cat outside her window was no ordinary cat. He did the normal things cats did, but in a slightly abnormal way, as if he'd read about cats in books and was trying very hard to act like he thought cats acted. He cleaned himself, like all cats, but he did it by dipping his tail in a bucket of soapy water and scrubbing himself with it. He sang, like cats did, but before singing at the moon, he'd hum his way through several sets of warm-up scales, and instead of howling tunelessly, he'd yodel arias and operettas that Marietta thought were rather too complicated for a cat, even a terribly clever one.

But today, *this* Sunday where our story begins, Marietta decided she was tired of letting him pretend to be a cat and decided to trick him into revealing himself. She'd been watching for several hours now, taking notes as he licked himself dry again, after toppling off the fence a couple more times for no reason that Marietta could see. She listened to him gargle his way through his scales, and just as he drew a deep breath, preparing to bellow out the first notes of the evening's selection, she opened her window and called to him.

"Kitty, would you mind moving your performance to another fence? It's a school night, and I need my sleep."

The cat, startled, bowed its head a bit and started to move away.

"Ah ha!" shouted Marietta, cocking a finger at the cat who had frozen in fear. "You understand me! I knew you weren't an ordinary cat. Who are you?"

The cat turned toward her and meowed hopefully in a very ordinary way.

"Too late," said Marietta. "I already know you're a fake."

The cat hissed and the fur on his back stood straight.

"Nope. No good. What else have you got?"

The cat yowled, it purred, it swiped at shadows and even jumped down to investigate something rustling and shuffling below, but each time Marietta just shook her head and smiled. "Come on now, who are you really?"

The cat lay down on his back, and a moment later there was the sound of a zipper, and the tip of a conical hat stuck out of the cat's belly. There was a great deal of struggling and pulling, and twice the cat fell off the fence. Finally, there was just the wizard, sitting on the fence, holding a cat costume in one hand and looking rather foolish.

"I knew you weren't really a cat," said Marietta. "You just didn't act like one."

"What did I do? Or what didn't I do?" asked the wizard. "You should never have noticed I wasn't a cat. I don't understand." He shook his head and smiled at Marietta. "None of the other children figured it out."

"Cats lick their whiskers, they don't wipe them with a napkin. And they sharpen their claws on the furniture or someone's leg, not with a nail file. And really, Sir, you ought to know that cats *eat* birds, they don't sing duets with them. Could you tell me, though, how so much of you fits into such a little cat?" asked Marietta. "You were cat-sized, which is very clever" (the wizard looked bashful but pleased at this), "but now you're human-sized, if a bit small."

"Oh, it's nothing," said the wizard, feeling warmth in his face, "Nothing at all, really. You just have to know the right words to say and where to put your knees." The wizard was feeling quietly hopeful. This girl, with her emerald-green eyes full of intelligence and excitement, was the most promising child he'd seen yet.

"I wish I could learn to do that," Marietta said. "I'd put on that costume and hop from fence to fence and climb trees faster even than Billy-down-the-block. I'd climb right to the very top," she sighed, looking from her window to the top of the fat oak. "That's what I'd do, if I could do that."

Again the wizard felt a dart of hope in his stomach. She sounded adventurous. She seemed brave. And a wizard climbing out of the stomach of a cat hadn't sent her screaming into the night. That was promising. The wizard stroked his beard.

"You are, perhaps, a rather-more-clever-than-ordinary little girl, I hope?"

"My mother says so."

"Yes, well, mothers do, don't they? What does your teddy bear say?"

"My teddy bear? I'm too old for teddy bears," Marietta answered.

"Then who's that lying on the pillow behind you?" asked the wizard, pointing.

"Well," said Marietta, blushing a bit, "I have a teddy bear, but I don't play with him anymore." She did, actually, but she felt rather foolish about it. "Besides, teddy bears can't talk."

"Have you ever asked him a question?"

"No, I don't think so."

"Hmph!" grumped the wizard. "Perhaps you're not so terribly clever after all."

"Where I come from, teddy bears don't talk, even if you ask them questions." Marietta didn't want to be rude, but her feelings were rather hurt.

"And how often do people hide inside cat costumes?"

"Perhaps they do all the time," said Marietta, who really didn't believe that at all. "Perhaps they're just better at it than you are."

"Humph! Indeed. Well. Perhaps they are. Now, if you'll bring your teddy bear to the window, we'll settle this question of cleverness."

"Even if he could talk, and I'm not saying he can, but just saying that maybe he could, why would you ask him about me? Why not ask my friends or my teachers?"

"Because, young lady, no one knows you better than your teddy bear. Who have you told more secrets to? Who do you cry with and have adventures with? Who follows you to sleep every night, if not your teddy bear? Now please, I have a lot more howling and hissing to do tonight; could you kindly bring your bear to the window?"

Marietta, feeling slightly foolish and terribly curious, brought her bear to the window.

"What's his name, please?" asked the wizard, all business and serious, grown-up face.

"Mr. Scrumpf."

"Is that with a p-h or an f?"

"Pf. S-C-R-U-M-P-F. It's the noise Daddy's nose makes when he sleeps."

"You named your best and greatest friend after a snore? Really, young lady, that shows some lack of respect. Now, ask your friend Mr. Nose Noise if you're a clever girl or not."

Feeling really terribly foolish now, Marietta put the question to her bear, and was very surprised indeed when Mr. Scrumpf answered.

"Far more clever than most," he said, and winked one of his button eyes even though Marietta could have sworn he had no eyelids. She nearly dropped him in fright, but then she remembered that he was her very special friend, eyelids or no eyelids. She hugged him, and for the first time in their long acquaintance, he hugged her back.

"I could use your help," said the wizard. "Things have been very strange in Incunabula – that's the place I come from – very strange indeed, and . . . perhaps you could help me?"

"Will you show me how you fit in that cat costume?"

"That and many other things besides. I'm a wizard, you see."

"I know," said Marietta, matter-of-factly. "I could tell by your hat." She kissed Mr. Scrumpf good-bye and placed him gently on the bed, then she jumped out the window and climbed up onto the fence. The wizard took her little hand in his not-much-bigger one, shut his eyes, and wished them away to Incunabula.

Chapter Three

When Marietta opened her eyes, the world she was in was quite fuzzy and blurry, but that was just because she'd had her eyes closed, and it soon cleared. The wizard's hand still held hers tightly, and his face was a bit green with white around the edges.

"Are you all right?" asked Marietta, who knew that green and white are not good colors for a face to be.

"Urrgl glaaslkkorph," answered the wizard, and he fell over into the grass.

Marietta was frightened for she liked the clumsy little wizard, and she didn't know what was wrong or what to do with him. But a moment later, the wizard sat up, and the patches of green were smaller, and the white was almost gone entirely, replaced by a much healthier-looking pink.

"What happened?" asked Marietta, helping the wizard to his feet.

"I don't like travelling," said the wizard. "It makes me sick. You don't feel badly at all, I hope?"

"No," answered Marietta, feeling almost guilty for feeling fine.

"I'll be right as rain in a moment. Or as right as rain can be, for in my experience, rain usually goes from top to bottom and not right to left at all. But perhaps on Earth it's different?"

"I don't think it means right to left," said Marietta, uncertainly.

"Perhaps not," said the wizard, and he spoke no more about it. He set off walking, stumbling almost immediately over a rock and falling down again.

"Maybe you're not quite ready to walk yet." And Marietta helped the wizard to his feet again.

"Oh, I'm fine, I fall down a lot. That's why they call me the tumble-down wizard." He searched in the grass for his glasses, found them, and set them back on his nose. "I'm a scribe: I write down what happens here, what I see and what I discover. That's my profession."

"You said there were odd things going on here?" Marietta looked around. So far, this Incunabula looked quite a lot like home. Trees grew up and not down, and they were brown at the bottom and green at the top and bigger than the birds who perched on their branches. The sun was yellow and there was only one. She had expected to find things very different, and now she was beginning to wonder if she'd left Earth at all. But just then, a Planter walked by, and Marietta suddenly knew this place was just as different as she could have wished.

Planters are creatures who grow different kinds of seeds all over their bodies. Farmers hire them to come to their fields and shake themselves so that seeds fly off and land on the soil. The only problem is that the farmers can never be sure what plants will come up, but it doesn't really matter. Every seed that is shaken from a Planter grows into something pleasant to eat or pleasant to look at, and often both together. They are in great demand during the planting season, and they spend hours walking through freshly plowed fields, shaking themselves as hard as they can and spraying seeds up to fifteen feet away. By morning, all the seeds they shook off the day before have been replaced, which makes them a very useful resource and well worth the special hot, humid tents that the farmers must build for the Planters to sleep in.

The wizard saw Marietta gaping at the Planter, so he explained what the creature was, just as I have explained it to you.

"Does it hurt?"

"Shaking off the seeds, you mean? No, I don't believe so. I've never heard one complain, anyway. Then again, I've never actually heard one talk at all." He scratched his chin, brought out his notebook, scribbled himself a note, and promptly tripped over the tattered end of his robe. Marietta helped him up for the third time, thinking that perhaps she'd be spending a lot of time hauling him to his feet, and she might as well get used to it.

"So what exactly is happening here?"

"Incunabula is infected with the Creeping Nasties."

"The Creeping Nasties? What's that? Or who?"

"It's a disease that's turning all the nice things about Incunabula into nasty things. I've even heard that the purest-hearted and kindest princess in all Incunabula recently kissed a toad — and it stayed a toad! Plus, she now has a horrible, ugly wart on her bottom lip." The wizard shook his head in despair, nearly losing his balance.

"Yuck. What causes it? The Creeping Nasties, I mean."

"The children of Earth no longer believe in us, Marietta, and so Incunabula is sick. We need the belief of the children of your world. They lend us their imaginations, and we use it for building materials, you see? Without the dreams and fantasies of Earth children, none of this can exist. Has any adult in your world ever accused you of 'building castles in the sky' when they caught you daydreaming?"

Marietta sighed. "All the time."

"That's because the grown-ups on Earth have some memory of Incunabula still left in the childish parts of their brains. They know, deep in their bones, that when children fantasize about castles in the sky, a real, solid, stone-and-mortar castle appears here in Incunabula. We used to have millions of them — so many castles in the sky that the dragons could barely fly between them. The castles used to bump into one another like boats on the water. Oh, it was a wonderful sight, Marietta. But now a castle in the sky is as rare as a six-footed land worm."

"Six-footed land worm?" Marietta repeated in disgust. "I think maybe I'm glad they're rare."

"Mmmmm," said the wizard, not really listening, his eyes intent on the empty skies.

"How do you expect me to help you?" asked Marietta. "If it helps, *I* believe in Incunabula."

The wizard looked at her and smiled, a little sadly. "Then that's a start," he said. "Can you build a castle for my sky?"

"How do I do that?"

"Dream it. Imagine it. Craft it in your mind like builders craft with their tools. Build me a castle, Marietta; I'd so love to see a castle in the sky again."

And so Marietta tried. She closed her eyes and imagined castles, all the castles she'd seen in picture books or in films, all the travel slides of castles she'd had to sit through when her aunt and uncle came back from Europe. She thought about white castles and brown castles and castles of brick and marble and wood, but when she opened her eyes, the sky was still empty except for a Daft Bird who had been startled by sunlight.

"I guess I'm as bad as all the other Earth children," she sighed. "I can't do it."

"Don't think about castles you know, think about castles you don't know."

"Think about something I *don't* know?"

"You do it all the time! You think about all kinds of things every day that you know nothing about. You think about stars and planets or negative numbers (really, how *can* you have two of nothing?) or particles so small you can't even see them. You learn about foreign countries in school, don't you? But you've never been there, so can you really know them? *Imagine*, Marietta. Let your mind play and see what comes out."

Marietta looked at the wizard's sad, scared face and realized, with a start, *He's afraid his world is dying. If I can make him a castle, he'll have cause to hope again.*

And so she closed her eyes, and this time she thought of huge, straight towers with pink marshmallows on top to help the building float in the air. She thought of archways colored like rainbows and doors that never opened because it was so much more adventurous to enter and leave through the windows. She thought of the kinds of foods that people in such a castle would eat: they'd have to eat light foods so as not to weigh the castle down, so perhaps they'd eat things like popcorn and angel-hair pasta sweetened with powdered sugar. They'd eat those wonderful chocolates that melt in your mouth and drink fizzy drinks with bubbles to keep the castle aloft.

Yes, that was the kind of castle she'd like to live in. At all times of day and night, light, lovely music could be heard in every room and corridor of the castle, and it was this music that made the castle lighter than air. Anyone with a heavy or serious thought had to get in a hot air balloon immediately and travel to the ground, for enough of such thoughts could make the castle heavy enough to crash. No one who lived in the castle ever wanted to leave, so too-ponderous thoughts were banished before they were fully born, and the castle was full of light of every color and many that haven't been named yet. The more she thought, the easier the thinking became, and she went on and on, adding new rooms and filling the castle with wondrous inhabitants until a voice at her side woke her from dreaming.

"It's beautiful, Marietta! Open your eyes and see!"

And it *was* beautiful, as beautiful as it had been in Marietta's mind, every detail copied from her fantasy and turned to life. It floated and bobbed in the air like a cork on water, and many happy faces were visible from the windows of the castle. They smiled down at the people below and waved.

"Thank you, Marietta! It's *wonderful!*" they cried, their voices so light they almost didn't make it to the ground.

And they floated away, leaving a trail of laughter behind them. Just before it disappeared from sight, the castle slowly rotated, and Marietta and the wizard could see three hot air balloons, ready to take away anyone whose weighty thoughts threatened the marvelous castle in the sky.

Marietta, stunned, turned to the wizard. "*I* did that?"

"Indeed you did, my girl, indeed you did. And now I know I made the right choice. Such a wonderful castle," he mumbled, turning and walking on, "Haven't seen a castle like that in who-knows-how-many years. Marietta!" he suddenly cried, turning back to her and almost falling over.

"Yes?"

"Good for you!" He threw his arms up to release some of the joy that was building up inside him. "What an absolutely *wonderful* castle!"

Chapter Four

The wizard decided it would be best to explore the bits of Incunabula that hadn't yet experienced the horror of the Creeping Nasties. It was important for Marietta to fall in love with this world so that she would fight as hard as she could to save it. With this in mind, they headed off to meet the Rainbow Maker.

Getting to the Rainbow Maker's workshop was not an easy task. They had to cross through the territory of the Chestnut Trolls and then climb Runaround Mountain which could take days as there were dozens of paths leading this way and that, and finding the right one was nearly impossible. At the top of Runaround Mountain was an elevator up into the sky where the Rainbow Maker had his workshop.

The Chestnut Trolls lived on the flatlands of Incunabula where chestnut trees grew in abundance. They ate their chestnuts fried, baked, boiled, broiled, steamed and marinated, or, as a special treat, they had chestnut ice cream with chestnuts on top. They drank chestnut milk and built their houses from chestnut shells. Everything the trolls required came from chestnuts, especially (and unfortunately for anyone in their path) their entertainment.

The Chestnut Trolls loved to sit in the low branches of their trees, throwing chestnuts at anyone who walked below. They would even fill their mouths with chestnuts, and then shoot them off like bullets from a gun: *ptooi! ptooi! ptooiptooi!* There was really nothing nice at all about these Trolls, and it was generally agreed that one could live one's entire life quite happily without ever meeting a Chestnut Troll. At the borders of the flatlands, just out of range, were the umbrella and hard-hat sellers, and they did booming business. It was madness to enter the domain of the Chestnut Trolls without some kind of protection, and the umbrella and hard-hat sellers could charge whatever they liked.

At the boundary of the flatlands, the wizard stopped and bought two hard-hats. The umbrellas were nice for shielding your entire body, he explained to Marietta, but they just couldn't hold up in the long run. The wizard and Marietta were going right the way across the flatlands, and umbrellas would be tattered and useless long before they reached the other side. He also bought a bottle of ointment for bruises, and they walked carefully into the land of the Chestnut Trolls.

It is really difficult to hold a conversation with chestnuts rattling off your helmet, Marietta thought to herself a few minutes later. *I wonder why the people here put up with this?*

They walked for half an hour, wading through chestnuts up to their knees, chestnuts flying in all directions around them, and many making painful contact. The thunking and bonking of chestnuts hitting her helmet was giving Marietta a nasty headache, and her temper grew shorter and shorter. Finally, she'd had enough. She picked up a handful of chestnuts and started firing back. The trolls were so startled that someone was throwing chestnuts at *them* that, for a moment, the rain of chestnuts ceased. A great howl of indignation went up from the trolls in the trees, and one very loud voice shouted at them from a bushy chestnut tree on their left.

"What are you doing?!" screamed the troll, obviously very angry, for his branch was shaking and quivering. "You can't throw our chestnuts back at us!"

"Certainly I can," answered Marietta, firing one directly at the voice and getting a satisfying *yip!* in response. "If you're going to throw things at people, you'd better be prepared to have them thrown back at you." She shot off two more chestnuts at two other shimmying branches and got two more *yip yip!*s for her efforts. She was glad she'd spent so many hours in snowball fights and softball practice, for her arm was strong and her aim was true.

The few others who had ventured into the flatlands also began scooping up handfuls of chestnuts and flinging them into the trees. Pretty quickly the trolls regained their senses and started chucking them back. The Great Chestnut War has been badly exaggerated in Incunabulan history books. In fact, the conflict lasted less than half an hour, not the fourteen days and nights the historians claim. And no one was killed or even badly hurt, although the wizard's bottle of ointment made quite a few rounds after the truce was declared. And Marietta's Army, as they came to be known, were badly outnumbered and soundly defeated. But they'd given the Trolls a taste of their own medicine, and soon thereafter the Trolls took to making sculptures from their chestnuts instead of throwing them. The real losers seemed to be the umbrella and hard-hat sellers, but they quickly adapted, turning the area into an art exhibit and charging admission, and making endless documentaries about the Trolls which they would show for a fee.

Once they got through the flatlands, Marietta and the wizard found themselves at the foot of Runaround Mountain. The climb looked easy, but in fact, they climbed up and down, this way and that way, over rocks and under trees, they tiptoed round corners where Giant Fuzzballs snored in their sleep, they chose this path and that path, and every path took them round and round, but they got no closer to the top. Asking directions was no good, for nearly everyone on the Mountain was as confused and lost as they were. Those who lived on the Mountain appeared to know the way up, but they gave directions more tangled than Marietta's hair or refused to help at all without the proper paperwork and authorization.

Marietta and the wizard ate berries and mushrooms they found on the trail, they ate dried biscuits from the wizard's backpack and drank from the clear streams that didn't seem to come *down* the mountain but rather from somewhere else entirely. It was the most confusing place Marietta had ever been in, and she became more frustrated and angry with every path that seemed to go up but really didn't. The Rainbow Maker chose to put the entrance to his workshop here because he didn't really like visitors, and Runaround Mountain discouraged all but the most dedicated guest.

As they climbed, Marietta noticed that every so often, there would be a flash of falling light nearby, a brightly-colored comet speeding towards the ground. These flashes came in many different colors, now red, now green, over there a streak of blue or a marvelous zip of orange.

One fell just beside Marietta, a shiny yellow one that exploded on the ground next to her feet. Just as Marietta was about to ask the wizard what they were, a whole river of bluish-purple splashed down from the sky and poured over the side of the mountain. The rattling noise they made reminded Marietta of the time she had broken a necklace, and all the beads had dropped to the floor.

The wizard looked at the sky and smiled a bit. "The Rainbow Maker is clumsy today," he said, and he grabbed her hand. "Lucky for us! Follow the color, Marietta; run towards the source!" And they began to run up the side of the Mountain, against the stream of color. They ran, stumbling, and reached the top just as the last few drops of purple fell from the sky. And there was the elevator that would take them to the Rainbow Maker's workshop.

Perched on the highest rock at the peak of Runaround Mountain was a big basket, much like the baskets that hang below hot air balloons. Tied to the basket was a rope. The other end of the rope was tied to a cloud, way up in the sky. The wizard went to the basket and gave the rope a sharp tug. A few more colored comets that had lodged in the cloud came rattling down around them.

The wizard, who had spent nearly as much time falling *down* the mountain as he had climbing *up* it, clambered awkwardly into the basket, tangling the end of his robe around his knees and finally landing head-first, feet-last in the basket.

"Bother," he said, uncrumpling his sadly crumpled hat. "Come along, Marietta, into the basket."

Marietta wasn't sure if a basket anchored to a cloud was the safest basket to be in, but she knew a trip into the sky couldn't fail to be exciting, so she hopped in. The wizard tugged the rope a second time, and the basket began to rise.

Seconds later, the basket bumped up over the edge of the cloud, and they climbed out. Directly in front of them was a glass door which read: *Roy G. Biv, Rainbow Maker*. The wizard opened the door, and they went in. The Rainbow Maker was not at all what Marietta expected, though she had had no idea what to expect.

He was a thin man, with a long, dark face the color of the chestnuts Marietta was still pulling out of her hair, and a long, dark beard, spattered here and there with gray. He sat on a small stool, stringing colored beads onto fishing wire. All around his workshop were pots full of beads, separated by color.

One pot had been overturned, and several bluish-purple beads lay scattered about. Marietta realized with a shock that these beads, falling from the Rainbow Maker's workshop, were the flashes of light and color she'd seen on Runaround Mountain. Mr. Biv had a very serious face, but not an unpleasant one, and he spoke like a man with a great deal of work to do.

"What do you need, Wizard?" he asked, tying the end of the fishing line to an arc-shaped, chicken-wire frame. "I haven't much time for your falling-down foolishness; spring is my busiest time of the year."

"This is Marietta, Roy. She's come from Earth to help us stop the Creeping Nasties. I thought perhaps she should meet you."

The Rainbow Maker gave Marietta a long look. Then, quite unexpectedly, he smiled a smile that lit up the whole workshop. His manner probably didn't make him very popular most of the time, but his smile set all the glass beads in their rusty pots a-twinkle. "Welcome, Marietta."

"Thank you. Can I ask what you're doing?"

The Rainbow Maker laughed, and his laugh was so bright, even people on the mountain below had to shield their eyes in the sudden glare. "Making rainbows, my dear. What else would a Rainbow Maker do, do you suppose? This one I'm working on is for the Kingdom of Spires. They're celebrating their 950th anniversary, and they've ordered a double-rainbow for Thursday: two full arcs, solid color all the way to the ends." He leaned forward a bit. "Confidentially, most want a strongly-colored middle, but a fade-out on both ends. Costs less, you see? And I haven't had a request for a pot of gold in, goodness, at least two hundred years now. Even the Irish have given them up."

"The Irish? But the Irish are Earth people," said Marietta, confused.

The Rainbow Maker laughed his laugh again, and the Chestnut Trolls slapped chestnut shells over their eyes to keep from being blinded.

"Bless you, child, *every* world has its Irish. I string my beads on this invisible wire, you see? Then I tie the strings to the frame, and I use those pulleys and ropes to lower the rainbows into position. I'm afraid I'm a bit behind right now, though. The Rainmakers and the Sundancers have finally called a truce in 50/50 Valley, and they've ordered a whole splash of rainbows to celebrate. But if you're going to fight the Creeping Nasties, you're going to need a bit of help."

With that, he stood up and brushed beads from his clothing. Marietta was astonished at how tall the Rainbow Maker was – regal and elegant as a prince.

He went around to each of his pots, selecting one perfect glass bead of every color to string on a bit of fishing line. Red, orange, yellow, green, blue, indigo, violet, and when he was done, he fastened the string around Marietta's neck.

Then the Rainbow Maker laid his hands on Marietta's shoulders, and he looked into her eyes. "At the bottom on the other side of Runaround Mountain is a weatherwoman who tells yesterday's weather because she thinks we should learn from our mistakes. I listen to her every day, and every day I learn something new by learning something I already knew. So I guess I learn something K-N-E-W, you see?"

"Sort of," said Marietta, who didn't see at all, but thought she might if she had time to think about it.

"Good," said the Rainbow Maker, sitting down again on his stool and dipping his hand into a pot of cool green beads. "Now go save the world. And while you're at it, could you stop in at the Dragon Forge and order me some more beads? I'm running low on indigo."

All the way back down to the top of the mountain and down the mountain to the flatlands and across the flatlands to another range of mountains, Marietta said very little. She had a great deal to think about: rainbows made by hand and creatures who grow seeds on their skin and wizards who could crinkle and fold their bodies to the size of a cat. There was so much magic here that you could feel it brushing past your skin and sitting in your hair like snowflakes.

But the Creeping Nasties were slowly sucking the magic out of Incunabula, replacing it with dull, unpleasant things. Not horrible things, not always, just the sort of ordinary, uninteresting things that threaten to clutter up a life the way knickknacks clutter a shelf, smothering what was beautiful and fun and curious and exciting with what was plain and tedious and necessary and useful. Ugh.

That couldn't be allowed to happen, Marietta decided firmly. Incunabula stored magic like power in a battery, and without its magic, it would be as flat and lifeless as a dead battery or a burnt-out lightbulb.

Marietta turned to the wizard to tell him of her decision to accept the fight against the Creeping Nasties, first helping him out of a giant mud puddle that he'd gotten muddled in (and nothing can muddle faster than a mud puddle muddles, as we all know). But just as she opened her mouth, something caught her eye. Her mouth opened all right, but in shock. No words came out. She was at the foot of Quiet Mountain, perhaps the most beautiful place in all of Incunabula.

Quiet Mountain is a very tall mountain, so tall that even if you crane your head so far back that you can smell the backs of your knees, you won't be able to see the top of it. The top is waaaaaay up, caught in the clouds, surrounded by blue sky, muffled in snow and silence. The rest of the mountain is a lush, green paradise with the biggest, brightest flowers and the sweetest smell.

It's called Quiet Mountain because even though it's a volcano, it never erupts or roars, never spills lava or shoots hot rocks from its top. It explodes only once a year on the Queen of Quiet Mountain's birthday, and then the volcano shoots fireworks and confetti and chocolate candies and presents. But the rest of the year, it sits still and quiet, gently rumbling to itself as it sleeps.

The palace of the Queen of Quiet Mountain is about halfway up the eastern slope, but it's an easy walk across fields of prairie grass tall enough to tickle your nose; through thick, dense forests of pine trees greener even than the green beads in the Rainbow Maker's pots; over brooks that not only babble but chuckle and chortle and giggle and often laugh out loud; and along winding paths that don't try to lose you the way the paths did on Runaround Mountain but rather try to show you the nicest views and the pleasantest places to walk. Yes, Quiet Mountain is a glorious place that fills your heart until it bubbles and fizzes and turns six kinds of somersaults, but most glorious of all is the Queen's garden.

The flowers in the garden of the Queen of Quiet Mountain are very special flowers, for they don't grow from seeds or bulbs like flowers on Earth. The flowers on Quiet Mountains grow from thrown kisses. Did you ever wonder what happens to a kiss once it's thrown? Where does it go? Well, now you know: it turns into a flower on Quiet Mountain. Throw someone a kiss, *mmmmmmwah!* and you've grown a giant daisy with bright yellow petals. And once you know this secret, you can decide how your flowers will look. I'll throw you a purple lily on a long green stalk: *mmmmmmmmmmmmmm* (that's the stalk growing) *WAH!* (that's the flower bursting into blossom). I've even engraved your name on one of its petals.

Millions and millions of flowers grow in this garden, flowers of all shapes and sizes, all smells and colors. A few are rather horrible, appearing when Mom makes little brother throw a kiss to his sister, for example. Then the flower is often black and prickly and smells of old cheese, but there aren't many of these. Marietta and the wizard walked around the garden for hours, looking at beautiful flowers and funny flowers and some very odd flowers (one had an eye in its center, and watched everything they did).

"When will we meet the Queen?" asked Marietta.

"Oh, we won't," answered the wizard. "No one ever does. No one ever has, or at least not for a very long time. She never comes out of her castle, and she never allows others in."

Just then, a fat, red rose burst into blossom just beside the wizard, exploding with so much love that it actually blew up and showered them both with red rose petals. The perfume of the flower was so strong that they both started to cough and gasp for air. They hurried away to another part of the garden.

"Young love," mumbled the wizard, pulling handfuls of rose petals from the pockets of his robe, "is a very messy business."

"Why doesn't she come out of her castle? Is she hiding?"

"Not hiding," said the wizard, "waiting."

"Waiting for what?" asked Marietta, picking rose petals from her hair.

"A very special flower. She once had a lover; he was an Ambassador from . . . oh, I forget where, but a place where they haven't got any flowers. He came to try to make a deal with her — she has so many flowers that his country thought perhaps she could spare a few. But she couldn't, you see; any flower that is taken from the garden immediately dies. They can only survive here on Quiet Mountain."

"And this Ambassador and the Queen fell in love?"

"They fell so hard that they may still be falling. They were a perfect pair. They had their wedding here in this garden, and the flowers never looked so beautiful or smelled so sweet. But just as the ceremony ended, the Ambassador was called back to his country because they had gone to war. The Queen swore she would go into her castle and never come out until he came back to her. He promised to throw her a very special flower so she would know that he was on his way. That was nearly four hundred years ago, and still the flower has never grown."

"She's waited four hundred years? That's stupid."

"Stupid? To wait for love?"

"Well, wait for love, sure, but do you really have to lock yourself inside your castle over it? She could have had four hundred years of adventures, four hundred years of making friends and doing things, and she chose to sit in her castle and wait for a flower? What a waste! Really, fairy tale women do the stupidest things sometimes."

The wizard looked thoughtfully at the castle. Behind one thin curtain, you could just see the outline of a head, its eyes fixed eternally on the garden. "Hmmmm," murmured the wizard, pulling at his beard, "I never thought of it that way. It always seemed very romantic and sweet to me, but perhaps you're right. Perhaps there's a better way of passing the time until her loved one returns."

"I could think of a thousand better ways without even trying," grumbled Marietta. "And what's *he* been doing all this time, huh? How long does it take to throw a kiss, just a little kiss to let her know that he still loves her and he isn't dead? Maybe he's not even worth waiting for. Maybe there's half a dozen flowers here from kisses he threw to somebody else."

"Yes, well, he did come from a place where the people aren't known for their constancy in love, that's true. I never thought of that before either. Really, Marietta, how can you stand here without a romantic thought in your head? Surrounded by all this love, still picking passionate rose petals out of your ears?"

"I'm a kid," said Marietta. "Romance is for sissies."

And with that, they turned around and headed back towards the entrance to the garden. Just as they started to open the heavy, iron gate, they heard *mmmmmmmmwah!* come from a high window of the castle, and a single white rose on a pale green stalk grew slowly from the ground just in front of Marietta.

"*Take it with you!*" called a gentle voice from the castle. "*I can help you, Marietta, but only if you take this flower with you.*"

Marietta broke the stalk of the flower and put the blossom in her pocket. She blew the Queen a purple forget-me-not in thanks, and she and the wizard left the garden together.

Back at the bottom of Quiet Mountain, the wizard handed Marietta a small notebook.

"These are all my observations about the Creeping Nasties," he said. "I hope they'll be useful to you on your journey."

"Aren't you coming with me?" Marietta was suddenly afraid. How could she fight them on her own?

"No. I can't do that, you see. I'm needed elsewhere, to keep track of the changes the Creeping Nasties have made so someday, hopefully, we can change it all back again. Keep your mind open, Marietta, and make friends where you find them. I have faith that you'll find a way to make Incunabula healthy again."

"But where do I go? How do I start?"

"You start *now*, and you go *on*. That's all I know. Good luck, Marietta."

And before Marietta could speak, the wizard pulled his hat down over his body and disappeared. Marietta was alone at the foot of Quiet Mountain with a flower, some beads, and a notebook from a tumble-down wizard.

"Wonderful," said Marietta, out loud. "Thanks for all your help, everyone. How about a map and a sandwich?" With a vast mountain range behind her and a great unknown land before her, Marietta was beginning to recognize the value of maps.

No one heard her and no one answered. Marietta closed her eyes, and spun in a circle, and when she was finished spinning, she started off walking whichever way she happened to be facing. It was the worst choice she could have made.

Chapter Five

In the Land of Infinite Variation, there was at least one of everything, and two of the more interesting things. Edgar the shape-shifting goat shared his burrow with an eagle who was afraid of heights and a lion that only ate carrots, and when they sang songs together (as they often did after tea), the notes formed bright lights that hung in the air for many seconds before exploding in tiny cascades of glitter and sparkles.

Everyone was terribly different from everyone else, but no one teased or made fun because in the Land of Infinite Variation, you could never be sure that when you woke up in the morning you wouldn't have a green nose or a belly button on one cheek or rather more arms than you'd fallen asleep with the night before. They kindly complimented each other on their appearance, just as we might when our friend has had a haircut:

"I do believe that extra nose is just the thing you were lacking," they'd say. Or, "What a perfect place to put an ear! How reassuring to hear your own heartbeat and know you're still alive. I wonder no one's thought of it before?" Friends frequently failed to recognize each other, and would happily make new friends with old friends, thus doubling their number of companions with a comfortable guarantee of compatibility.

It was a gentle place where beautiful and ugly were measured on the inside and not the out, and the only people who laughed at others were those who had gotten the Giggles and couldn't help it anyway.

The Land of Infinite Variation lay just to the south and east of the Empire of Cheese. Well, it didn't always *lay*, really; sometimes it sat, or stood, or slumped to one side, or just sort of *leaned* against the Empire of Cheese, and it wasn't always to be found to the south and the east. Sometimes it was a tiny bit north or a very wee bit west, and often all four together, which confused even the cows.

The Emperor of Cheese tried very hard to separate his Empire from the Land of Infinite Variation, but it was an impossible task. Everything that touched that Land was vulnerable to it, and the Emperor's fences would be iron and steel one day, and strings of buttercups the next. One morning his great fence disappeared altogether, reappearing eight days later with a broad smile and refusing to say where it had been. The Emperor knew when his cows had crossed the border into the Land, because they would come back with the head of a lion or a moo that sounded like a foghorn and nearly blew all the other cows out of the field. Instead of producing milk, they might produce candlewax or butter-rum candies or, in one memorable case, some very startled elves.

He railed and complained and tried to pass legislation to force the residents of the Land of Infinite Variation to register the number of fingers they had and the color of their noses and what parts of their bodies they walked on or spoke through or thought with, and to make it illegal to vary even in the smallest degree with their registered identity. But none of these things worked, of course; he passed his law, but the next day it turned into a law requiring all three-toed dingo-riders to tell purple riddles on alternating Globsdays, and since such creatures *never* follow rules, it was ignored and soon vanished completely. No, the Emperor of Cheese had no luck at all trying to win an argument with anyone in the Land of Infinite Variation, he just had to learn to put up with cows whose horns played classical music and who would, for no reason at all, suddenly start wearing lipstick and dancing the tango.

Had Marietta gone to the Land of Infinite Variation, she would have spent many happy hours watching ears grow where there had been no ears before, or listening to camels who suddenly had voices for the very first time, or placing bets on who would be the next person to lay an egg from his armpit. But she didn't go there. Had she gone to the Empire of Cheese, she would have tasted many fine cheeses (those not yet contaminated by the Creeping Nasties) and comfortably listened to the Emperor rant about his neighbor to the south and east (or north and west or over there or just around the corner or wherever his neighbor happened to be at the time). But she didn't go there either. Marietta, when she finished spinning, set off in the direction of the Great Cratered Cobweb, an unfortunate decision if ever there was one.

The Great Cratered Cobweb wasn't really a cobweb, it was a section of land so pockmarked by craters, the land in-between looked like a giant cobweb. Some of the craters were immensely deep, the deepest being the Bottomless Pit of Falling Paul. This crater was named for Paul, an unfortunate boy who had one day stumbled and fallen into the crater, and since the pit was bottomless, it was assumed he was still falling. At the beginning of every week, the elders of a nearby village would go the edge of the Bottomless Pit to sing songs of soft landings and throw in loaves of bread and bottles of water tied to bricks. It was hoped that these would fall faster than Paul, so he'd have something to eat and drink on his way down. Since he'd started falling nearly a hundred years ago, they now soaked the bread in milk first, just in case he hadn't any teeth left.

The other craters, while not as deep, were generally just as nasty and many contained very unpleasant surprises at the bottom. In one crater was a spirit gum mine where spirit gum was chipped from the rocks and hauled up to the surface in baskets. On Earth, spirit gum is a sort of sticky glue that actors use to glue fake beards and moustaches to their faces; in Incunabula, it's used to glue restless spirits inside their bodies.

Some spirits are not meant to live inside bodies – they fly and race between the stars, they dart in shadows and swim like fish in the air – and to be imprisoned in a body is a terrible punishment for them. If you ever meet a person who is terribly restless, always jumping up and bouncing around, chances are this is a spirit that's been glued into its body and is trying to pull itself free.

Marietta wandered into the Great Cratered Cobweb completely by accident, not realizing at first what a very horrible place it was to be in. Sometimes the land between the craters was so thin, it was like walking across a tightrope, but Marietta could balance like a cat, and this didn't bother her much. What bothered Marietta was the silence. This place was a very silent place, so silent that Marietta caught herself breathing in a whisper. So irritating and depressing was the silence that finally she coughed out loud, and the echo of that cough, swirling around the bowls of the craters and spilling over into other craters only to be stirred around some more, came back at her a thousand times louder than when it had first emerged from her throat. Then she understood the value of silence in this place, and she stifled her coughs in her hand from then on.

She avoided looking too deeply into the craters; every time she caught a glimpse at the depths of one of the pits, something stirred, something with too many arms and too many teeth and the wrong kind of smell. Things scurried into shadows just a bit too quickly for her to see them. Things rustled and shuffled and muttered here, and Marietta didn't like that at all. She vowed to move as fast as she could to get out of this place, but just as she made this promise to herself, a croak of despair caught her ear. This sad, almost-hopeless cry had come from the bottom of the spirit-gum mine, and without another thought, Marietta slid down the slope of the crater to help whoever needed it.

The bottom of the crater was very very dark, and the floor was so sticky that she had to keep moving or be stuck fast forever.

"Where are you?" she called quietly, afraid of the echo. But she needn't have worried; her cry stuck to the spirit gum walls and went no further.

"Is there someone there?" asked a voice both sweet and brittle, like a frozen chocolate bar.

"Where are you?" Marietta called, a little louder. "Keep talking so I can find you."

"Keep talking?" said the voice, and Marietta was surprised to hear the faint trace of a smile. "Well, that's easily done. Talking is something I do rather well," the voice continued, and Marietta followed after it. "I talked ice cream into melting on a hot day, and I convinced night to be dark, and I once persuaded a nightingale to sing."

"But all those things happen normally," said Marietta, gingerly feeling the walls of the cavern with her hands. Every time she pulled her hand away, a bit of the wall stuck to her fingers and she had to rub it off. The spirit gum was sticky and greasy and cold, and Marietta rubbed frantically to get it off her skin.

"Well, *now* they do," said the voice, "but who do you think told them that they should?"

"I can't find you," said Marietta. "Keep talking."

"Very well," said the voice, "but my strength is almost gone. The miners will be back soon to chip more spirit glue from the walls and laugh at me, stuck here and helpless."

"They laugh at you, they don't help you?" asked Marietta, shocked almost to tears. "That's horrible!"

"This is rather a horrible place, if you hadn't noticed," came the croak from off to Marietta's left, "and horrible things happen here on a daily basis. Which is good, in a way, because if they happened somewhere else, then *that* place would be horrible instead of nice and lovely, and that would be too bad for the people who lived there. Yes, best that the horrible things happen here where at least the people expect them. Have you found me yet, young lady?"

"I'm close, by the sound of your voice, but all I've found are what feels like some old feathers."

"Then you've found me, my dear. I'm a bird. And please don't pull that too hard, I need it to steer with."

"Oh!" cried Marietta, pulling her hand away, "I'm so sorry! I didn't realize that was you. Please forgive me."

"Not at all," said the bird. "I'm sure you didn't mean to."

"Now that I've found you, how do I get you loose?"

"You don't, I'm afraid," the bird replied. "Spirit glue is forever. But thank you for making the effort; it's so nice to have someone to talk to, even for a moment."

"Isn't there anything I can do?" asked Marietta, who felt so unhappy for the bird her feet sank three inches into the glue on the cavern floor.

"Be careful, my dear. Sadness makes you heavy, and heaviness will stick you in the glue. Have you ever had gum on the bottom of your shoe? Then you know how impossible it is to get off, and spirit gum is a thousand times stickier. The only way to free someone imprisoned by spirit glue is to give them a red bead from the Rainbow Maker, but his workshop is many days walk from here, and before you could get there and back, my life would be exhausted."

"But I *have* a red bead!" Marietta cried, joyfully, and she untied the cord with shaking hands and pulled the red bead loose. "Here! Quickly!"

"But what if you get stuck? No, I can't take it. You may need it to escape from here. Which you should probably start doing. Escaping, I mean. The miners will be back soon, and they won't be happy to find you here."

"What do I do with the bead, to free myself? I mean, just in case I need to know."

"You swallow it like a pill," said the bird, and his voice was much weaker now. "The red heat of it melts the spirit gum, and you can fly free. Well, if you're a bird, you can fly free, anyway."

"My goodness, I'm suddenly so sleepy," said Marietta, and she yawned noisily.

In Incunabula, just as on Earth, yawns are contagious, and of course the bird yawned deeply as well, just as you're doing right now. His wings were stuck fast to the walls, so he couldn't cover his mouth, and as quick as a flash, Marietta dropped the red bead in. The bird coughed a bit, but the bead went safely down his throat, and a moment later, he glowed red enough to illuminate the entire cavern. Marietta saw him pop free from the wall and flap his wings frantically to keep from falling to the gummy floor. Too exhausted to fly, he landed heavily on Marietta's shoulder.

"Hang on tight," she told him, and she started to run. Well, she meant to start to run, she *tried* to start to run, but her feet were stuck fast to the floor, three inches deep in gum. And they could hear, just below the rim of the cavern, the sour song of the gum miners returning to work.

"You wonderful, foolish girl," the bird croaked in her ear, "you sacrificed your only bead on me. And I'm too tired to fly, and your feet are rather too firmly on the ground, and now that I've been given a second chance to live, I'd rather not die in this awful place. What shall we do? If the miners find us here, they'll throw me against the wall again, but at least we'll be able to talk together for as long as our lives last."

"Don't give up yet," whispered Marietta, very quietly for the miners were fast approaching. "We'll think of something."

But their time had run out. The miners had come back to the mine, and though Marietta couldn't see them, she could hear them. They were close by. Marietta struggled to pull her feet free of the gum, but she was stuck fast. The miners were coming closer; she could hear the metallic rattle of shovels and buckets as they returned to work.

"Can they see in the dark?" Marietta whispered to the bird.

"No. They are blind as moles," said the bird. "They feel vibrations, so stand as still as you can."

There was a miner in the cavern with them. Marietta could hear him rustle as he moved. She stood as still as she could, but suddenly everything wanted to tremble and shake and quiver. She held her breath and clenched her teeth to keep them from rattling in her head. The bird on her shoulder was so still, Marietta wasn't sure if he was even there anymore. The thump of the pickax was so sudden, Marietta nearly jumped out of her shoes. The axe made a sharp, ringing sound that was quickly muffled by the glue. And that sound was getting closer.

"He's coming this way," said the bird, in a voice so small Marietta *felt* it more than she *heard* it. Something, an idea, was playing at the back of Marietta's mind, but she couldn't quite get ahold of it. The noise of the axe was getting closer as the miner mined gum in a circle around the edges of the cavern.

pingwhomp! pingwhomp!

Something about being scared . . . of course! She'd nearly jumped out of her shoes! That was it! She quickly squatted down and untied her shoes. Her motion must have caught the miner's attention, for the sound of the axe stopped. Marietta, still crouched on the floor, heard the miner take a deep sniff. He was looking for them. And Marietta had a knot. Frantic now, not knowing when she would feel a calloused, greasy hand grab her in the darkness, she tugged at the knot, pulling it tighter. The miner was inches away, she was sure of it – he was zeroing in on her, soon soon soon!

Almost in a panic, Marietta yanked so hard that the shoelace snapped. She quickly pulled off her shoes and, feet free, she ran. Blind in the dark, she ran towards what she hoped was the way out, the miner's fingertips just brushing her as she fled past him.

With her new friend anchoring himself in her hair, she darted barefoot and quick-like-lightening past the startled miners and up the steep slope of the cavern to safety. The next few moments were occupied with laughing and hugging and kissing with relief.

Once at the top, Marietta and the bird had their first chance to look at one another. The bird was small, about the size of an Earth robin, but he was absolutely black save for one white feather on his breast. His eyes were black and friendly, and Marietta trusted him immediately.

"My name's Marietta," she said, feeling a bit awkward about introducing herself to someone she'd hugged and kissed only a moment before.

"I'm called Shadowlark," the bird replied. "I'm really a terribly troublesome companion, but I'd like to go with you wherever you're headed. I'm often in need of saving, and it would prevent a great deal of fuss and bother if I just rode on my heroine's shoulder, if you see what I mean. Much less waiting around, calling for help and all that."

"Just as you like," answered Marietta, glad to have found a friend.

Chapter Six

The Shadowlark was indeed the best and most troublesome of friends. He gave Marietta good advice and rode quite comfortably on her shoulder, always careful not to dig his sharp claws into her skin, and his wings were handy in an emergency, but because of his shadowy nature, he could live only on the boundarylands between light and dark. Too much light, and he would become like one entranced, flying higher and higher to discover the source of the light. Too much dark, and he disappeared into the shadows, overwhelmed by his own mysteries and the darker side of his nature. At either of these extremes, he would vanish for days, only to reappear in the boundarylands, weary and ragged as though he had fought with a thousand demons and lost as often as he had won.

Marietta was always afraid that one time the Shadowlark would simply not return. So, to keep the friend upon whom she depended, she learned to walk the tightrope between light and dark, never allowing the balance to tip enough to lure the Shadowlark away.

"Where do you go when you go?" she asked him once.

"Up or down, depending on the light or the darkness," he replied, munching purple berries and hiding the seeds in her hair.

"What does that mean?"

"I know you're not that foolish," said the Shadowlark. "Down is where you go when you fall, up when you fly. But then you're an earthbound creature, aren't you. Sometimes I forget."

Marietta was rather put off by this comment. "I know up from down, thank you. And stop planting seeds behind my ears, please."

"When you start combing berries out of your hair, perhaps you'll remember to wash behind your ears more often."

"You haven't answered my question, Shadowlark. Where do you go when you leave me?"

The munching just beside her ear stopped for a long moment. "Perhaps it is something like dreaming is for you," said the Shadowlark, quietly. "You go where you're taken. It's much the same for me." He started to eat again, this time spitting his seeds at the ground.

"Do you like one better than the other, light or dark?"

"Do you prefer dreams to nightmares?"

"Of course."

"Well, there you are then." And he crunched quite determinedly in her ear and would answer no more questions. And Marietta walked the tightrope between light and dark with even greater care from that day on.

Because much of Incunabula was fairly shadowy anyway, it wasn't all that difficult to stay in the boundarylands between light and dark. In fact, the more the Creeping Nasties took hold, the darker and more shadowed the light places became.

Neither Marietta nor the Shadowlark had the least idea how to defeat the Creeping Nasties. The effects were everywhere, it seemed, and Marietta was beginning to give up hope that there was anything she could do about it. She read a little more from the wizard's notebook every night, but it didn't help much. He didn't just write about the Creeping Nasties, he wrote about all Incunabula, and his descriptions of wondrous places made Marietta sad to think that they could be destroyed. But one place the wizard mentioned in his notebook turned out to be extremely important indeed: the Land of the Moon-Shadow Tigers.

Mirror Lake lies at the foot of the Rock-Topped Mountains beneath the Towering Waterfall. It is called Mirror Lake, because at night, the moon looks directly into its waters to smile at its own reflection. Anyone who seeks to call the Moon-Shadow Tigers must go to the lake in the dark of night, and stare into the depths of the water. If their heart is pure and their need is great, when the screech bird screeches the first time, the Moon-Shadow Tigers will appear. The seeker must be very brave indeed, for the tigers will kill anyone who calls them down from the sky for a useless or cowardly purpose. But once the tigers deem the seeker and the need to be worthy, they become the best and most loyal friends anyone can have.

Marietta knew that the Moon-Shadow Tigers were important in her quest to defeat the Creeping Nasties. Shadowlark tried to talk her out of going to Mirror Lake, because the tigers were huge and ferocious, and a single swipe of one huge paw could quickly rid the world of a green-eyed, black-haired little Earth girl and a raggedy, shadowy bird. But Marietta insisted. *The tigers can help*, she said, over and over. *I feel it in my heart.*

When they reached Mirror Lake, Shadowlark flew up high to the top of Towering Waterfall to keep watch. In truth, he was terribly nervous and chose not to be where fangs and claws might appear.

Marietta leaned close and looked into the shining surface of the water, just as the moon pulled itself free from the bony fingers of the highest peaks of the Rock-Topped Mountains. The screech bird echoed its first screech through the leaves of a hanging-bariat tree. She looked and she looked, and for the longest time, nothing happened. But then, a single ray of moonlight, trapped on the earth when a cloud moved over the face of the moon, broke free and shone full and bright on the water, and Marietta could see them just over her shoulder: two white faces, so big and white, whiter even than the face of the moon.

She turned around slowly, her long, black hair just sweeping the surface of the water. Marietta's green eyes looked into the fierce brown eyes of the Moon-Shadow Tigers, their faces only inches from hers. She was afraid, and her blood beat through her veins hard enough to make her whole body shake, but she could not look away from them. Finally, a few seconds or perhaps a whole lifetime later, the screech bird screeched a second time, and the Moon-Shadow Tigers curled themselves into a gleaming, silver-white circle at her feet.

Even lying down, the tigers' heads were far above Marietta's own, so huge were they. Their breathing was a quiet rumble like a train passing many miles away.

"So the wizard has brought you to rescue this land from its disease?" asked one tiger, his voice a soft but powerful murmur much like distant thunder.

"Yes," Marietta whispered. She was almost afraid to speak aloud. The tigers were so beautiful – the glossy, ivory whiteness of their fur crossed with stripes darker than the best-kept secret; even without touching them, Marietta knew that no fur had ever been softer or thicker or worn with more pride – they were so beautiful that Marietta couldn't believe they were real, and she was afraid that with one harsh noise, she would awaken, and the rest of her life would be spent grieving for a lost dream.

"The task is difficult," murmured the other tiger in a voice slightly softer and lighter, more like the tumbling waterfall behind them.

"I don't know what to do," Marietta admitted. "The wizard said that Earth and Incunabula are separating, and that Incunabula is starving for the imagination of Earth children that feeds its magic."

"Our scribbling wizard knows many things, Marietta," said the first tiger. "He can estimate the kilowatts of each star in our sky and trace the family history of every creature on the soil or under it, but his understanding is limited."

"Where does fire come from, and where does it go when it dies?" asked the second tiger, flicking the ground with her tail and causing dust-storms a hundred miles away. "Why does moonlight make shadows and sunlight chase them away? What does water say to water when a cloud rains into the sea? The wizard doesn't always ask the right questions, and he only finds a true answer when he stumbles and falls over it in his tumble-down way."

"I don't understand," said Marietta, shaking her head.

"The wizard is a good man who doesn't understand what evils can hide in the heart," said the tiger on the right, the one Marietta thought of as *he*. "Yes, Incunabula is being starved. But on purpose."

"Who is doing this? Who could be that cruel?" Kill this beautiful, wondrous place on *purpose*? Why?

"The culprit is the dream-stealing Dark Prince of Dullardry," said the left-hand tiger, and her voice cracked and rolled like the thunder of an approaching storm. "We don't know exactly how he does it," she said, moving slightly and crushing a boulder to powder beneath one careless paw. "Only that the more Incunabula changes, the faster it changes, and the more powerful the Dark Prince becomes."

"How do I stop him?" asked Marietta, determined that he *would* be stopped, and quickly.

Shadowlark had been quietly watching from one of the peaks of the Rock-Topped Mountains, and as no fang or claw had yet made an appearance, he decided it was safe to fly down and join the conversation. He flew (a bit painfully and none too gracefully as many of his feathers were still rather sticky and hard to control) along the path of the Towering Waterfall, and came to rest on Marietta's shoulder.

"Recovered from your tiger-fear, Lark of Shadows?" rumbled the he-seeming tiger, sitting up.

Shadowlark was so startled at being addressed by the tiger that he accidentally clutched too hard on Marietta's shoulder and sank his claws deep enough into her skin to draw blood.

"I'm sorry, Marietta!" he cried, and he flew to Mirror Lake, dipped the tips of his feathers into the water, and flew back to Marietta to clean her wound. The minute the water touched her skin, Marietta felt different, *changed*. She felt as though something deep within her had shifted slightly and fallen into place. A warmth flowed from her shoulder down her arm to tingle in her fingers and then flowed through the rest of her body, making her feel as though a rose were blossoming inside her, unfurling petals kept too long in a tight bud. She felt strong and confident, more than she ever had in her life. Incunabula, it seemed to her now, was more real than the three-bedroom, brown-and-green house she'd left behind on Half-Circle Drive in a small town in another land so far away that even memory could barely reach it. The she-seeming tiger nodded, as if she understood what Marietta felt.

"You're one of us now," rumbled the tiger. "From now on, Incunabula is within you, just as it is in all of us. Truly, Shadowlark," she said, turning her massive head slightly to peer at the trembling bird on Marietta's shoulder, "you are the best and most troublesome of friends." She turned back to Marietta. "The magic of this land has flowed into you through the water that mixed with your blood. But it makes you vulnerable to the disease just as all of us are."

The tiger on the right studied Marietta for a long moment. "Are you afraid?" he asked, finally.

"Yes," Marietta whispered. She wasn't sure if what had just happened to her was the best or the worst thing that could possibly happen, but she knew she was afraid of the disease. *Everyone* was afraid of the disease.

"Good," answered the tiger, to Marietta's surprise. "Fear will make you careful. Find the Dark Prince and defeat him, and perhaps Incunabula can yet be saved. But be alert for symptoms of the sickness within. Search for the wonderful; don't be distracted by the merely colorful. Fight for the impossible; don't settle for the safe."

"I will," Marietta whispered, "I promise."

The she-seeming tiger reached out one giant paw and plunged it deep into Mirror Lake. She flicked out a long, silver fish and flipped it up onto the shore where moonlight glinted on its scales. A moment later, the fish had become a gleaming silver sword.

"Take it, Marietta," the Shadowlark whispered into her ear.

She bent and picked up the sword; she swang it a few times, experimentally, liking the weight of it in her hand and the singing noise it made as it cut the air. She swang it a few times more, with greater confidence, before sliding it under her belt.

"Tigers," she began, struck suddenly by a thought, "if everything an Earth child imagines comes true here in Incunabula, why can't I just wish the Dark Prince out of existence or change him into a puddle or imagine his castle tumbling down on his head?"

"The Dark Prince isn't one of us," said the he-seeming tiger, "and so he's not subject to our laws. Find out where he comes from, and you'll find the source of his strength."

"And where he is weak," said Marietta, her hand on the hilt of her sword.

"And where he is weak," the tigers agreed.

Just then, a patch of clouds moved across the face of the moon, covering it almost completely. A single ray of bright light shot through a gap between the clouds and landed at the base of the Towering Waterfall. When the hole closed and the moonbeam was gone, so were the Moon-Shadow Tigers. Marietta hadn't even seen them go.

"We'll see them again," said Marietta as she started to move away from Mirror Lake.

"Yes, I rather think we will," sighed the Shadowlark. "Teeth and claws and all."

"Where now, Shadowlark? I seem to get all kinds of new information, but what I really want to know is which direction to point my feet."

"I have a question for you about feet," said Shadowlark. "Why don't they wear down? Shoes wear down, and tires on carriages – why not feet? You put so many miles on them, poor waddling things that you are."

"Shadowlark, not everyone is blessed with wings, but that doesn't mean you have to be a sky snob. Walking is a perfectly respectable way of getting around."

"Certainly it is, if you don't mind the slow, plodding trudge instead of the graceful, wheeling arcs of flight."

"Shadowlark, you are the most infuriating, ridiculous creature. . . ."

Still arguing, they set off from Mirror Lake, destination unknown.

Now, geography books may sometimes seem horribly dull and pointless to you, but when you are in an unfamiliar place, they can be very helpful indeed. They tell you where the water is and what's good to eat and when you might expect to bump into a mountain or fall into a valley or trip over a river, and which places are best avoided and why. They provide information about the people who live there and what animals lurk in the trees, ready to pounce, and whether you'll need a warm jacket or not.

As much as she hated the subject at school, Marietta would gladly have traded a year of her life for an Incunabulan geography book to tell her where she was and if the natives were friendly.

[Sadly for Marietta, no Incunabulan geography book has been written for several thousand years, thanks to the Land of Infinite Variation. Because the Land moves about when no one is looking, turning deserts into desserts, glaciers into girdles and seas into cheese, geography books were constantly having to be rewritten, and serious geographers felt silly marking places that used to have sensible mountains as now having big piles of string and some spoons. This issue was once discussed at a conference of geographers, but in the middle of a very important meeting, the Land bumped up against the conference hall, turning it into a giant heap of underpants from which the geographers had to fight their way free. No conferences have been scheduled since.]

Marietta's job was to find the kingdom of the Dark Prince of Dullardry, but she had no map and no geography book to show her the way. She and Shadowlark traveled for days, asking everyone they saw if they knew the way. No one could help them, but everyone had a Creeping Nasty story to tell. Unicorns' horns were becoming soft and rubbery like old carrots, and some of them had fallen off entirely. One man who had a genie in a bottle woke up one morning to find that the genie could no longer turn himself to smoke to get free of the bottle. He was stuck in there, sulking, until someone could come up with another idea. Fizzy drinks had lost their fizz, and instead of sending bubbles up your nose, they were more likely to shoot paperwads or peas. The Nasties were getting nastier, there was no doubt about it.

"I understand," Marietta told them when they came to her with their hands full of fear and tried to stuff it in her pockets. "I need your help to fix it. Please, can no one tell me where the Dark Prince of Dullardry may be found?"

"Why don't you try the Office of the Promises General?" muttered the Parliamentary Secretary of Satisfying Sneezes whose nose had fallen off that morning. "He's a pretty dull fellow, if it's dullness you're looking for." He scraped the last of the spirit gum from Shadowlark's feathers and used it to stick his nose back on. Marietta didn't have the heart to tell him it was upside-down. She just hoped he wouldn't drown the next time it rained.

With the Shadowlark perched on her shoulder, happily munching purple berries, Marietta went off to meet the General of the Office of Promises. She found a tall, square building so uniformly dull and boring that if the Creeping Nasties hit it, no one would notice.

The sign on the door read, "Office of Promises, Official Residence of the Promises General – Important Business Only, please, as we are really very busy and silly interruptions make us cross. Thank you." Marietta decided that her business was important enough, so she pushed open the door and walked in.

Inside the hallway of the building were two more doors, one to the right and one to the left. The door on the right had another sign, this one reading, "Office of Promises Made – Promises Broken Division." Marietta opened the door to peer in.

Inside, it was an absolute beehive: people rushed about scribbling things on bits of paper, reading other things on other bits of paper, making long lists in huge, fat books five times the size of the most endless history book ever written. They shouted names at one another and listened on telephones (two or three at a time, sometimes; the more ears you had, the better chance you had of getting a job here, and some creatures had so many ears that Marietta couldn't help thinking that perhaps any amount over ten was ridiculous, really). It was so noisy and frantic in here that Marietta backed out of the room and shut the door, relieved to be in the quiet of the hallway. The door on the left also had a sign, and this one said, "Office of Promises Made – Promises Kept Division." Marietta figured this room would be the same as the other, but she gently pushed the door open, just to make sure.

It wasn't. This room was quiet. Silent, in fact. One man sat alone at one desk, a tiny notebook in front of him, and a single pencil lying, sharp-pointed, just to the left of the notebook. A thick layer of dust covered it all, including the man. He sat very still; so still that Marietta wondered if perhaps he was a statue, until he sneezed, quite violently.

"You stirred up the dust," said the man, in a voice that creaked as though covered with rust.

"I'm sorry," said Marietta, and they stared at each other in silence for awhile. Shadowlark, full of purple berries, had crawled under Marietta's hair for a quick snooze, and his quietly raspy breathing was the only noise in the room.

"That's OK," the man said, finally, "It's the first thing to happen here in ninety-four days." He spoke slowly and carefully as if he were searching through the dusty, musty files of his brain for the proper words.

"Oh," Marietta responded. She wished she had more to say because that *oh* kind of bounced and bumped around this empty, silent room before coming to rest on top of the man's desk. "It's very quiet here," she said, and it was very quiet again for a long moment.

"Yes."

"What do you do here?" asked Marietta.

"I keep track of promises," the man answered. "That is, the ones that are kept. That's my profession. Mostly I twiddle my thumbs, though; would you like to see?"

Marietta didn't, not at all, but she said she did because she wanted to be polite. The man brought his hands up to the desktop and twiddled his thumbs furiously for a moment.

"Once I twiddled them for one hundred and sixty-six days without stopping. That's an Incunabulan record. But no one noticed. I would have kept on twiddling, but I got a cramp."

"You're very good at it," said Marietta, who was always polite to grown-ups, but she had to struggle not to laugh.

"It's not a very useful thing to be good at, I know," said the man, "but I've nothing else to do. So few promises are kept, you see. The last promise kept was . . . ," and here he consulted his notebook, "made by Captain Maplewood who promised that he'd kill the ogre that lived in the hills or die trying."

"And did he kill the ogre?"

"No, he died trying, but it still counts. How many days is it 'til Christmas?"

"I don't know," said Marietta, startled. "Why?"

"Never mind, it's just that I must prepare my list for Santa Claus. He's my biggest client, you see."

"Oh, really?"

"Certainly. They say that he makes his list and checks it twice, but really it's me who does all the compilation of names and the cross-referencing."

"I see."

"I've heard rumors that we provide information to an even more illustrious client," and here he pointed meaningfully at the ceiling, "but I suspect that may be an exaggeration of sorts."

Marietta nodded her head to show that she was paying attention, then suddenly shook it so hard that she nearly shook the Shadowlark off entirely – he had been dozing quite comfortably under a blanket of her hair.

"Whazzat? Whashapnin? Whazzamattasumpin?" mumbled Shadowlark, still mostly asleep.

"Something is happening to me!" Marietta whispered urgently to the dozy bird on her shoulder, "This man holds records in thumb twiddling and he's so dull he bores holes in the walls, yet I can't tear myself away. It's like going into a trance! He keeps talking, and I keep listening. What can I do to get free of him?"

"Don't panic!" hissed the Shadowlark, now completely awake. "And don't fall into the rhythm of his voice, or you'll be frozen here forever. Really, Marietta, it's quite ridiculous to fight the Chestnut Trolls and come out alive from the bottom of a spirit gum mine only to have your life sucked out of you by the very first Dullard you meet."

"What's a Dullard?" Marietta whispered back.

"*That's* a Dullard," answered the Shadowlark, pointing one wing at the man who was drawing squares and circles in the dust on his desk with a yellow fingertip.

"If I had my way," the man said, suddenly, "I'd put the bathroom sink at the end of the bed. You could do all those horrible things like combing your hair and brushing your teeth and scrubbing those little nobbly bits from between your toes without having to get out of bed. Makes sense to me — another thirty minutes in bed every day. That's anywhere from fifty to three hundred extra hours of bedtime a year!"

(Incunabulan years are often a bit shorter than Earth years, but sometimes they're a bit longer and sometimes twice as long, and sometimes so short that people go to sleep in one year, wake up two years later, and discover they've missed everybody's birthday and have quite a lot of apologies to make. This is the result of an error that allowed the only calendar-making factory to be run by the Time-Wobble Elves of Emlin. The "TWEEs," as they're called, have a very different idea of time: to them, time is a game and should never be taken seriously. "How old are you?" is no longer considered a useful or even answerable question, and has been replaced by, "How old do you feel?" which most Incunabulans think is a more sensible question anyway.)

Marietta, who hated bedtime as a general rule, found herself nodding. She was rapidly falling under the Dullard's spell.

"Oh yes, so many extra hours for standing quietly in a corner or cleaning those wads of lint out of the corners of your trouser pockets or plucking the hairs from your ears. All those lovely, empty hours!"

"Please hurry and think of something, Shadowlark," Marietta whispered, and her voice sounded far away and very small, even to her own ears.

"Bother!" said the Shadowlark, who was starting to feel the spell of the Dullard as well, "I thought you'd be doing all the rescuing, and I'd just hang about being rescued. I'm no good at this hero business."

"The wizard's notebook!" Marietta murmured under her breath, "Quick, it's in my pocket. My arms have gone numb, so you'll have to get it out. See if there's something there that can help us."

Her energy was dissolving right out of her, like a can of soda going flat. Dullards feed on the energy of others, leaving them flat and dull and empty. Marietta was starting to think about taking a quick nap right there on the desk and then later on, maybe staring at a bit of the wall for awhile. She could feel the Shadowlark rummaging around in the pocket of her jacket, but it didn't seem that important anymore.

"Can you imagine my surprise when the knob on the bottom drawer on the left hand side of my desk came right off in my hand?" the man asked, watching Shadowlark trying to turn the pages of the wizard's notebook with his beak. "Oh no, you don't want to do that," he said to the bird. "That's very naughty of you. Hand me that notebook, and I'll put it in this drawer right next to my extra socks. I always keep a clean pair handy, just in case."

Marietta struggled desperately not to ask, just in case of what? Her head felt foggy and blurry, and the man's voice was hypnotic. She wanted nothing more than to stand very still for a *very* long time.

"You're probably wanting to ask, just in case of what? Well, I'll tell you: I suffer from this truly awful foot fungus-"

"I've got it!" croaked the Shadowlark. "Listen!"

The more the Creeping Nasties infect Incunabula, the more Dullards there are to beware of. These are the soldiers of the Prince of Dullardry's army, and they have spread far and wide across the land. Never get in a conversation with one – they can literally bore you to death. If you do, you must quickly think of something important: think of someone you love,

*something that makes you angry or happy or sad or excited, anything that
makes your heart beat a little bit faster. Focus on it for all you're worth.
Block out the voice of the Dullard, and you stand a chance of getting away.*

Marietta tried to get her heavy, sluggish brain to sit up and pay
attention, but nothing she could think of seemed exciting or important.
In fact, thoughts were emptying out of her brain so fast, you'd think
there was a fire in there.

"I have an emergency pack that I always carry with me," said the
Dullard, and his voice was lower and drowsier and more magnetic than
ever. "It's got lots of things that I might someday need. Shall I show
you?"

Marietta thought of Christmas and popcorn strings and fat stockings
stuffed with treats and eggnog and snow, but even brightly-wrapped
packages seemed pointless and boring.

"I've got a needle and thread — six different shades of brown, you
see? I always wear brown; I find it hides the dirt so much better . . . "

Marietta's heart was slowing to match the sluggish trudge of his voice
as it moved across the room. She thought of Halloween candy, of witches
and ghosts and things that went bump in the night. She thought of
masks and costumes and Jack-of-the-lantern, but even caramel apples
and midnight magic lay at the bottom of her brain, panting, like fish
out of water.

"I've got a candle here, and a box of matches in a plastic bag in case
it's a wet emergency like a flood or a hurricane or the annual Spitting
Contest of the Drooling Giants of Slobber Ridge. . . "

Mom and Dad . . . bedtime kisses . . . softball games in the park . . .
and . . . picnics and . . . checkered blankets . . . birthdays . . . birthdays?

"Now for your dry emergencies," the Dullard continued, his eyes
fixed on Marietta's, "like fire and earthquake, I've got hand cream. All
that dust and ash on your skin is *so* uncomfortable, I find. It might
seem silly, but in difficult times, these little things can make a real
difference . . . "

Something about birthdays . . . a special present this year . . . a you're-only-a-kid-once-said-Mom sort of present. What had she gotten? She couldn't remember . . . .

"I do like to keep some packages of peanuts handy. They provide a little protein, and they last forever in the packet."

A birthday puppy, that was it! Marietta's heart beat a tiny bit faster, a little smidge harder. The Dullard, as if perhaps he'd heard the changing beat of her heart, talked a bit louder in his lazy, droning voice.

"A pair of scissors. Vital in every situation. Who knows how long you might be trapped in a collapsed mine or under an avalanche? But that's no excuse for having split ends or your bangs in your eyes."

Marietta, catching hold of that tiny bit of her brain that was still awake, concentrated hard on her birthday puppy: his wet nose, his cottony soft fur that smelled of stored sunlight. The way he stuck his quick tongue in her ear and got muddy pawprints on her best clothes. More of her brain was listening in, paying attention, coming awake. She was shaking off the spell, coming back to *life*. Shadowlark, however, was completely under the Dullard's spell, and he fell from her shoulder to the desk with a heavy *thump* and was still.

Louder yet, faster, spoke the Dullard: "I've got gloves for every situation: warm gloves for cold places, plastic gloves for wet places, and gardening gloves for places that get under your fingernails. I've got six types of screwdriver, eleven sizes of nose-hair clippers in case I'm not alone, and best of all-"

"Enough!" shouted Marietta, breaking free with the happy thought of a golden puppy named Bumble who was afraid of thunder and who had chewed up those horrible, black, patent-leather shoes she hated so much. With one hand, she picked up the unconscious Shadowlark, and with the other, she grabbed her sword and brought it down hard on the Dullard's desk, breaking the desk in two. The Dullard stared at her, shocked.

"You mean . . . you mean you're not interested?" he asked, his eyes wide and hurt in his voice.

Marietta leaned forward over the ruined desk that was bleeding clean, brown socks and spools of brown thread and looked the Dullard directly in the eye. "Not at all," she said, and he crumpled into dust and blew away.

Cradling the still-dazed Shadowlark in one arm, Marietta turned to run out of the building. But someone was standing in the doorway. A very dark Someone. A very tall, thin, dark Someone was blocking Marietta's escape.

He leaned against the doorframe, picking his teeth with the bone of some small animal. He wore a suit so black that light seemed to fall into it; Marietta felt she was looking into a deep hole. He had a short black beard and long, thin fingers tipped with sharp black fingernails. He couldn't have been any more evil if he'd worn a sign around his neck that said, "have a horrible, pointless, rainy, stupid day, go to bed early without any supper, and cry until your pillow drips with tears."

Oh, he was evil all right. You could feel it oozing through his pores, and Marietta was sure he left a trail of evil behind him like a slug leaves slime. He sent shivers not only down Marietta's back but down both arms and both legs and around her neck and even through her hair until she felt she had an army of shiver-ants marching trails all over her body.

"You're the Dark Prince of Dullardry, aren't you?" she demanded, trying to make her voice sound strong and sure.

The evil figure in the doorway threw its head back and laughed that laugh that only really awful, nasty people can laugh without sounding ridiculous.

"That's right, Earthworm," he hissed, and his voice made the shiver-ants run even faster over Marietta's skin. "Catch me if you can." And then he was gone.

Marietta's hand tightened its grip on her sword. "I will," she said to the empty air, and she tucked the half-awake Shadowlark into one pocket. "And that's a promise."

Chapter Seven

Perfectly Frank is a liar. It's what he does best, and he's proud of his ability to lie about nearly anything from the color of the sun ("green with bits of yellow," he says) to the feel of grass beneath bare feet ("it stings," says Frank) to his own origin ("I was rumbled up to the surface of the planet during an earthquake," Frank claims, but in fact his very ordinary parents live on a farm not far from the village of Cabbage-on-Toast). He pretends that he is honest and tells nothing but the truth, but this is his biggest lie of all. The very first time he opened his mouth to speak, he said, "Now, let me be perfectly frank."

"OK," his parents agreed, "go ahead and be Perfectly Frank." And Perfectly Frank he has been, in name at least, ever since.

Fortunately for everyone else, Perfectly Frank is a terrible liar. Every time he lies, he giggles and sticks a finger in his left ear. Everyone knows this, so no one is fooled by his lies, and he generally doesn't cause much trouble.

The first time Marietta met Perfectly Frank, she was looking for a pair of shoes to replace the ones she'd left three-inches deep in the spirit gum mine. She and Shadowlark were on their way to the Handmade Village to request a pair of shoes from the Cobblers' Council. (The Cobblers of the Handmade Village make the finest shoes in all of

Incunabula, but they are very choosy about their customers. You have to prove that you will treat the shoes with love and kindness before you are allowed to adopt a pair of your own. There are endless forms to fill out, along with inspections and examinations. The average stay in the Handmade Village for those seeking shoes is twenty-eight days.) Perfectly Frank, on the other hand, wasn't going anywhere as he was, at that moment, tied to a tree.

"Hello," said Marietta, realizing that the tree she'd just passed by had a person attached to it. "Can I help you?"

"Oh, no, thank you," said Frank, giggling a bit and trying to free one of his hands. "Just getting some sun, you see," and he nodded his head at the thick cover of leaves and branches above them that kept all but the slenderest rays of sunlight from getting through. He jerked his right hand loose and stuck his thumb into his left ear, giggling all the while. "Is there something I can do for you?"

"I doubt it," said Marietta, looking at the thick ropes and tight knots that held him.

"You're Perfectly Frank, aren't you?" asked Shadowlark suspiciously. He'd heard of this character before.

"Oh no, dear me, absolutely not, wouldn't hear of it. Wasn't anywhere near the place. Dreadful-sounding person, this Perfectly Frank of yours. What did you say his name was again?" Frank would have collapsed into a pile of helpless giggles had he not been conveniently tied to a tree.

"He *is* Perfectly Frank," whispered Shadowlark into Marietta's ear. "Beware of him; he's the biggest liar in all of Incunabula."

"Frank," said Marietta, moving a bit closer, "why are you tied to this tree?"

"What tree?" asked Frank, who would have stuck his whole arm in his ear, if he could.

"The one you're tied to," answered Marietta, pointing.

"Goodness! I didn't even notice," giggled Frank. "Perhaps it's my birthday?"

Marietta began to laugh. Perfectly Frank was so completely ridiculous, he seemed to take away some of the weight that had been pressing on her heart. "Is this a common birthday present, then, to be tied to a tree and left alone in the forest?"

"Oh, certainly," said Frank, nodding his head hard enough to shake several acorns out of the branches above. "I rather expect my friends are off somewhere arranging marvelous surprises for me, and this tying-me-to-a-tree nonsense is just to keep me out of the way."

He eyed Marietta closely. "But *you're* not carrying a gaily wrapped present with a card that says, 'to Frank, in gratitude for his honest heart, with love from whoever-you-are.' Don't you know that it's my birthday?"

Marietta laughed even harder. "No it isn't, Frank. But since I've missed all your birthdays before this one, I'll give you a very special gift." She pulled out her sword and cut the ropes that held him. "There. Happy Birthdays, Frank. But you stay with me until I find out what it is you've done."

"Done? I've done nothing," said Frank, managing to look both offended and grateful at the same time.

"Hmmmm. We'll see. Now, which way to the Handmade Village?"

Perfectly Frank pointed one finger in a northerly direction and the other in his ear, so Marietta wisely turned toward the south. They walked for awhile in silence.

"Shadowlark," Marietta said after they'd been walking for some time, "what does the wizard's notebook say about Perfectly Frank?"

The bird untucked the notebook from under Marietta's collar and began flipping the pages with his beak.

Perfectly Frank [read the Shadowlark] *is perhaps the biggest rascal in all of Incunabula. He tells the truth only when the truth is unavoidable, and the number of times this has happened can be counted on one foot of a three-toed dingo-rider. He is, however, almost completely harmless.* [Here Frank snorted a bit as if insulted.] *He gives clear signals to indicate when he is lying, namely giggling and sticking a finger in his left ear. This happens with such frequency, it's feared that one day a finger will simply grow into his ear and have to be surgically removed.*

Frank may be an excellent measurement of how far Incunabula has been invaded by the Creeping Nasties. He is a sort of link between storytelling and outright lying, and as long as his lies remain imaginative and colorful, we know that Incunabula can still be saved. But if ever we find Perfectly Frank unable to tell his fantastic tales, we will know that the situation here in Incunabula is dire indeed.

"Ridiculous!" snapped Frank as soon as Shadowlark had finished. "Why, I've left such a trail of confusion and chaos behind me, I was recently given a medal by the Academy of Trickery and Falsehoods!" [This was actually true – he was awarded such a medal. Unfortunately for Frank, the people who gave him the medal and praised his lies were lying.]

"I would love to meet the kid who dreamed *you* up, Frank," said Marietta fondly. "What a troublemaker that one must be!"

Shadowlark's claws suddenly gripped Marietta's shoulder tightly, their signal that he had sensed something wrong or dangerous. Marietta grew more alert, looking intently into the thick green wood that grew on all sides of them.

"A shadow-bird, a teller of tales and a silly little girl from Earth. What a ragged band of heroes you are." The voice that Marietta would never forget shot out at her like a poison-tipped arrow from the shadow of some trees. "Did you know, Earthworm, that infected as you are by Incunabulan water, you can never go back to Earth?"

Cold panic hit Marietta in the stomach. "What?!"

"Why, yesssssssss, Marietta-of-nowhere," hissed the Dark Prince, emerging from the forest to stand in front of them. "No mummy, no daddy, no teddy bear or birthday puppy. Just a tattered, broken-down bird for your only friend." The Dark Prince shook his head. "Incunabula makes another orphan."

Marietta's heart would have sunk into her shoes if she had been wearing any, but she made herself stand straight and proud.

"Talk of my friends with respect, Prince of Afternoon Naps," she snapped, "or I'll-"

"You'll *what*, Earthworm?" and the Prince was suddenly no more than a few inches in front of her, his foul breath hot in her face. His mouth twisted with anger, all sharp, yellow teeth within. "You dare to threaten me? With that silly little toothpick you wear on your belt? I'd have expected more from the tigers, but perhaps they didn't have much faith in you and were reluctant to waste a good sword."

Marietta's confidence was so low, she was afraid she might step on it, but she forced herself to look the Prince in the eye.

"The tigers are my friends. To them, you're nothing more than rotten lunch meat."

"You've got a bug on your shoulder," the Prince said, and he reached up and grabbed the Shadowlark. He was so fast that Marietta couldn't stop him, and Shadowlark had only time to let out a startled croak before a gloved hand covered his beak.

"Let him go!" shouted Marietta.

The Dark Prince flipped the bird upside down and held him by his feet. Shadowlark flapped his wings desperately, trying to right himself, but he couldn't.

"Why, he's hardly more than a mouthful. What possible reason could you have for lugging this scrawny chicken around with you?" The Prince started to pull Shadowlark's legs apart. "Care to make a wish?"

In one quick motion, Marietta pulled out her sword and clipped off the tips of three of the Dark Prince's fingernails. He dropped the bird, and Shadowlark, shaken but unhurt, flew to perch again on Marietta's shoulder.

"Touch my friends again," Marietta warned, "and it'll be three of your fingers."

For a moment, the Dark Prince hesitated, and his whole body *flickered* like a movie reaching the end of the reel. There was something else behind . . .

"Give up the game, Marietta," said the Dark Prince, and his voice was low and heavy with poison. "Evil always wins. That's just the way of the world – your world and mine. Evil wins because it's more interesting. Who votes for boring old Good? Who would, when you have Evil to make life exciting?"

"Interesting theory from the Dark Prince of Dullardry," said Marietta, who was feeling rather braver now she'd seen that *flicker*. "You aren't evil. You're the King of Yawns in a sharp suit."

The Dark Prince was so angry that the air around him throbbed with his fury like a giant heartbeat. He grew bigger, and the sour smell of him made it difficult to breathe. Against this savage power, Marietta felt very small indeed.

"Guard your friends well, Earthworm," and his voice was crackling and hot and hit them like oil popping in a frying pan. "Your love for them makes you weak and vulnerable, and I will destroy them like *this*." He snapped his fingers under her nose, the sound loud enough to deafen her for a second.

"Those beads the Rainbow Maker gave you have protected you from me so far, but I will make you give them up. One at a time, you will sacrifice them all to save your friends, and with every one you lose, the stronger my hold over Incunabula will become. You've given me one bead already."

"What do you mean I gave it to you?"

"Who do you think threw the Shadowlark against the wall in the dark depths of the spirit gum mine? Oh, I'll take them all, Earthcrawler, and that's a promise. And when the last colored bead falls into my hands, Incunabula will be mine forever!"

"Incunabula will never be yours."

"The process has already begun. Much of this world already belongs to me, just as you, one day soon, will belong to me. My own Earth child. Perhaps I'll plant you in my garden and see if more Earth children will grow. The game is won. I would tell you to give it up and go home, but of course, poor child, you can't!"

He laughed again and disappeared into the depths of the forest, leaving only that wretched smell behind. Marietta's knees trembled so hard with anger and fear that she nearly fell. Frank, who had spent the whole time looking the other way and whistling as if he hadn't noticed anything out of the ordinary, put his hand on her shoulder to steady her. His unexpected kindness helped to calm her, but still her hand gripped her sword tightly.

When it became clear that the Dark Prince wasn't coming back, Marietta returned her sword to its sheath.

"Shadowlark," she asked the bird who crouched, shivering, under her hair, "is it true what he said? That I can't go home again?"

"I don't know, Marietta," came the quiet, raspy voice in her ear. "Perhaps the wizard knows."

Marietta stood without speaking for a long moment, thinking of a puppy named Bumble who had saved her life but who, perhaps, she would never see again. She thought of her parents, too, but that caused such a slash of pain in her heart that she quickly turned her mind away.

"We'll sleep here tonight," she said. She wanted time to think and to look through the wizard's notebook, but she fell asleep almost as soon as she'd settled herself on the ground, a soft lump of sweet-moss under her head.

At some point during the night, Marietta awoke to find the Moon-Shadow Tigers curled head-to-head and tail-to-tail in a protective circle around her and Frank and Shadowlark. Her eyes met those of the he-seeming tiger.

"Go back to sleep, child," he murmured. "We have a great deal to talk about tomorrow."

The warmth of their bodies and the soft rumbling purr of the she-seeming tiger quickly sent Marietta back to sleep. Tomorrow would come in its time.

Chapter Eight

When Marietta awoke the next morning, the Moon-Shadow Tigers were gone. She thought for a moment that perhaps she had dreamed them, but when Perfectly Frank sneezed himself awake, complaining that he had six ounces of fur in each nostril, Marietta knew the tigers had been there. A few minutes later there was a rustle in the brush, and the Moon-Shadow Tigers trotted into the circle where all had slept.

"Marietta!" one called. "Come with us, quickly!"

The she-seeming tiger bent down low to the ground, and Marietta understood that she was to ride on the tiger's back. As carefully as she could, she pulled herself up on the back of the beast. When the tiger stood up again, Marietta could feel the rippling strength of this powerful animal. *The ground must tremble with every step she takes,* Marietta thought.

The tigers leapt back into the tangle of the forest, and Marietta had to keep her head down to avoid being brushed off the tiger's back by low-hanging branches.

"Where are we going?" she asked, shouting to make herself heard above the roar of the wind and the crash of the forest being trampled under the tigers' feet.

"To the wizard," came the reply. "He isn't far."

"Why are we going to him?" she asked, as close to the tiger's ear as she dared.

"For an answer to your question," said the tiger. "If the waters of this land will prevent you from going home again, then we must know it now, before the infection spreads too far. We may yet have time to send you back before it's too late."

"But what about Incunabula? And the Creeping Nasties? I haven't done what I came here to do!" They were running so fast now that Marietta wasn't sure the tiger could hear her – her voice was caught by the wind and blown behind them before her words could reach the tiger's ear.

"Incunabula will find a way to survive, Marietta. We cannot ask you to sacrifice your home for ours."

The wind in her face brought tears to her eyes. Or perhaps the tears were already there, and the wind provided a convenient excuse.

"Please, stop. Please. There isn't time to find another Earth child." The words fell from her mouth before she even knew they were there. "Incunabula can't die. Not when I can save it."

The tigers slowed to a stop, and the she-seeming tiger lowered her head so Marietta could slip to the ground.

"Think carefully about what you're saying, Marietta. You could be trapped here forever."

"I don't believe that," said Marietta, and a quiet voice in her heart told her she was right. "I'll find another way back. Where there's love enough, there's always a way home."

"The decision is yours," said the he-seeming tiger. "But since we've come this far, we might as well consult the wizard."

Marietta nodded. She'd be glad to see the funny, clumsy wizard again, and perhaps he *would* have an answer for her. The she-seeming tiger bent her head down again, and Marietta climbed on. The softness of the tiger's fur, the sweet tiger scent of mystery and moonlight that surrounded her gave her confidence. She would get home again, in time, and she laughed out loud to think what Billy-down-the-block would say when he heard of her adventures. The last scrap of her troubles seemed blown away by the speed of the tigers, and she threw her arms open wide as they ran.

"Is this how it feels to ride on a moonbeam?" she cried to the tigers. "If I could run like this, I'd *never* stand still!"

This made the tigers laugh – a golden sound so rare that perhaps one person in a century gets to hear it. If the Dark Prince had been nearby to hear that wondrous sound, he would surely have slunk into the shadows, defeated, never to be seen again. Unfortunately, the Dark Prince was nowhere around, and his defeat was far from certain.

It would have taken Marietta four days to walk from where she had slept to where the wizard was busy scribbling in one of his endless notebooks. It took just four hours by tiger. The wizard was spending a few days with the Emperor of Cheese, documenting all the changes that the Creeping Nasties had brought about.

The Emperor of Cheese had very white skin, so white you could see the blue of his veins running underneath, and he smelled faintly of curdled milk. His royal robes were embroidered with cows: cows grazing, cows standing along a fence gazing into the distance; cows singing in little choirs and playing musical instruments; cows running six-legged races with two of one cow's legs tied to two legs of another cow; cows balancing eggs between their horns in honor of Dairy Day.

The Emperor loved cows, of course, and he spent hours with them in the fields, telling them his dreams of a great cheese palace and trying not to step in the cowpats. In this green land, to be called "cheesy" was considered the highest compliment, and the Emperor thought his cows very cheesy indeed.

But the Creeping Nasties had hit his empire hard, and the Emperor had called upon the wizard to try and stop the infection from spreading any farther. The wizard had been in the Empire of Cheese for several days now, and he'd taken pages full of notes, but no solution had as yet appeared.

The Emperor's marvelous cheeses had turned to gray sponges that didn't smell very good and tasted even worse, or to rough bits of sandpaper that would make your mouth bleed if you were foolish enough to eat them, or to gluey pieces of cardboard that turned your lips horrible colors and stuck your teeth so fast together that it took three strong men several hours to get your mouth open again. No one had bought so much as a single slice of cheese in weeks, and the Emperor was growing desperate.

The wizard was sitting quietly in one of the Emperor's fields, trying to see if he could spot the boundary of the Creeping Nasties, when the tigers suddenly appeared at his side. He had met the tigers only twice in his life, and, like Shadowlark, he was rather afraid of them. When Marietta climbed down from the back of one of those tremendous beasts, the wizard knew he had done well when he had brought her to Incunabula. No ordinary child of Earth would be invited to ride on the back of a Moon-Shadow Tiger.

"Hello, wizard," said Marietta, helping him up from the ground and righting the stool he'd fallen off of.

"I see you've met the tigers, then," said the wizard, straightening his robe, which was wrinkled and stained, and his hat, which was even more crumpled-looking than ever.

"We've a question to ask you, scribbling wizard," said the tiger on the right, and he lay down on the ground to make it easier to talk. "Marietta has been infected with Incunabulan magic. The Dark Prince claims that she'll never be able to return to Earth – do you know if this is true?"

"You've met the Dark Prince of Dullardry? Where did you find him?"

"We didn't find him," Marietta admitted. "He found us. But what about my question? Will I be able to go home again?"

The wizard looked thoughtful and scratched his head, knocking his hat to the ground and crumpling it still further. "I'm not sure. I'll have to consult my notebooks and the old records. It's quite an interesting question, yes indeed, very interesting." He stopped to scribble a reminder to himself in one of his notebooks, circling it twice and adding stars and exclamation points so that he would know it was important. Then, just to be absolutely certain he wouldn't forget, he tore the page out of the notebook and tucked it inside his hat which he then returned to his head.

"Is there nothing you can tell us now?" rumbled one tiger, in a rather louder-than-usual voice.

The wizard looked startled, and his face went a bit pale around the edges. "Nothing I can tell you for sure. There is an old Incunabulan legend about another Earth hero who came to save this land many thousands of years ago. According to the story, he too swallowed some of our magic." The wizard paused for a moment.

"And?" asked Marietta, her eyes bright.

"He . . . uh, I . . . I forgot," said the wizard. "And it's just a story, anyway; nothing to take too seriously, no, no. Not seriously at all. But there's another problem."

"What's that?" rumbled the tiger on the left.

"The Dark Prince. He's closing all the links. Many are completely sealed already, and the rest will be soon."

"What does that mean?" asked Marietta.

"Earth and Incunabula touch at many points," explained the wizard. "And at these points of contact are links between the worlds, doors and tunnels where humans and Incunabulans can cross."

"They can? And they do this? How come I've never heard of this place or met anyone from here?"

"Oh, it doesn't happen much these days," said the wizard. "Now that Earth doesn't believe in us anymore, Earthlings don't even see the links. They walk right past them without even noticing. A few have crossed: Lewis Carroll spent quite a lot of time here, as did Dr. Seuss. There's a link in your bedroom, actually," the wizard said to Marietta, "just to the side of your mirror. That's how I came across, one morning when you were at school. The problem is, once those links are sealed off, Incunabula is finished. No imagination can get through, and Incunabula will starve."

"Oh no!" cried Marietta. "We have to hurry! So what do we do next?"

"It's time to seek out the Dark Prince where he lives. We must go directly to his lair and challenge him," said one of the tigers.

"But no one knows where he lives," said Marietta. "I've asked everyone I've seen, and no one can tell me where to go."

"I've been thinking about that, actually," said the wizard, sitting down again on his stool and almost missing it. "There's a very old man who lives on Tumble Island, far up in the hills in a house called the Apex Pagoda. He's the oldest storyteller in all of Incunabula, and they say that every story ever told is somewhere in his library. Surely he knows where the Dark Prince came from, or perhaps the answer lies somewhere on his shelves. It might be worthwhile to ask him, at least."

"Tumble Island?"

"Yes, it's where I come from," said the wizard, blushing. "I suppose I should have thought of him before."

"Then we must go to Tumble Island," said the she-seeming tiger who had been busy cleaning herself after her run.

"What about the Shadowlark and Perfectly Frank?" asked Marietta. "I can't just leave them behind with no explanation. They must be quite worried about me by now."

"The Shadowlark will be here soon," said the he-seeming tiger. "He's been following us since we left the place where you slept."

"And in the meantime," said the wizard, "perhaps we can find you some shoes. Tumble Island is a very cold place – you'll need warm clothes. I wouldn't worry about Perfectly Frank, Marietta; he can take care of himself. No doubt he'll pop up somewhere in need of your help."

The trip to Half-Land, the place where the water meets the shore, took many days, even by tiger. Shadowlark had arrived in the Empire of Cheese completely exhausted from his long, painful flight – a ragged bird flies rather slower than a Moon-Shadow Tiger runs, after all – so now he rode on Marietta's shoulder, and she rode proudly on a tiger's back.

Marietta had a new pair of shoes, made by a Cobbler of the Handmade Village. The Cobbler had wanted Marietta to fill in the paperwork and sit for several examinations about proper shoe care and the history of shoe making, but one dark growl from a Moon-Shadow Tiger had sped up the process considerably. She also had a beautiful, thick, new winter coat to wear on Tumble Island.

The wizard rode uncomfortably and nervously on the back of the other tiger. They had to stop several times to pick him up off the ground after he slid from the tiger's back.

"His fur is so silky and slippery, that I slide right off it," he explained, by means of apology.

"Then I suggest you hold on tighter," growled the tiger, the fifth time they stopped to dust the wizard off and set him again on the tiger's back.

At Half-Land, the travellers stopped. Only Marietta and the Shadowlark would continue: the tigers had other matters to attend to, and the wizard wasn't allowed on Tumble Island after he had caused an accident in another wizard's laboratory. His clumsiness around powerful magic had blown off the top of the highest mountain and caused it to rain magic love potion on the Island for eight days after. People had fallen in love with rocks, with their breakfast, with bits of paper or a tree, whatever they set eyes on immediately after being doused with potion. Then more potion would fall, and they would find themselves deeply, desperately in love with the neighbor's cat or the bathtub, or their toothbrush, or a bag of marshmallow and coconut candy.

The tumble-down wizard had run all over the Island, distributing potion-proof umbrellas, but when the crisis was over, he was kicked off the Island and told never to return. He was still quite embarrassed about the whole thing.

"We weren't even trying to make love potion," he admitted to Marietta one night when no one else was listening. "That's the worst part of all. We were trying to find a formula that would protect people from the Trolls of Questionable Origin. We had heroes who had been *fighting* the Trolls suddenly *falling in love* with them! Really, you can't believe the mess."

Marietta couldn't help it. She laughed out loud at the ridiculous story and the forlorn expression on the wizard's face. "I'm sorry, wizard, but it's just so absurd! How long did the potion last?"

"Oh, days and days!" said the wizard, brightening. "It was a very good love potion. Unfortunately, the formula was lost in the explosion. Pity, really. The soldiers weren't very happy when they snapped out of it to find themselves serenading a bunch of smelly trolls, though." And then the wizard began to laugh as well, and pretty soon Marietta and the wizard were knee-deep in giggles and couldn't stop.

When they finally reached the shore of Half-Land, they could see the towering mountains of Tumble Island in the distance. (Well, one mountain didn't "tower" quite so well anymore, thanks to the wizard, but the other mountains towered quite magnificently.) It was much colder here, and Marietta was grateful for the new winter coat. They would spend one last night together, here on the shore, and then in the morning, Marietta and Shadowlark would hire a boat to carry them to the Island.

"The old Storyteller is a bit of a rough character," the wizard warned as they sat in a tight group around a fire. "He'll want something from you in exchange for any information. Have you anything to give him?"

"I have only the Rainbow Maker's beads, the notebook you gave me, and the flower from the Queen of Quiet Mountain. Will one of those do?"

"No," rumbled a tiger. "You shouldn't give up any of those. You'll need them to protect you."

"Then I've got nothing to give him," said Marietta.

They all sat silently and tried to think of a gift the Storyteller would accept. But they came up with nothing, and when morning broke, it was too late to worry about it. It was time to hire a boat, for the winter winds were coming, and once they started sweeping across the Divided Ocean (so called because when it hit Half-Land, half of the water stayed above the land and turned to lakes and rivers, and half of the water disappeared below and what it became, no Incunabulan knew), no one would dare take a boat out on the water for many months.

"You'll have to go and come back quickly," said the boatkeeper. "Winter is coming, and once it hits, no one will bring you back from the Island. Not for any price." The boatkeeper turned to look at the wizard. "You look familiar. Do I know you?"

"No. Impossible," said the wizard, and he pulled his hat down low over his face.

The trip from Half-Land to Tumble Island was rough and rather slow. The boat stubbornly pointed back the way they had come, the boatkeeper insisted that the boat point toward the Island, and their argument took the shape of sudden twists and rolling turns, sharp yanks and slow-motion swirls that would have turned most passengers a green to match Marietta's eyes.

Shadowlark crawled deep into one of Marietta's coat pockets, saying he preferred that his breakfast stay where it was, thank you very much, and within seconds, Marietta's pocket began expanding and contracting with the rhythm of his snores.

"What business takes you to Tumble Island at this time of year?" the boatkeeper shouted over the crashing waves.

"I need to talk to the Storyteller!" Marietta called back.

The boatkeeper nodded and fixed his eyes on the Island in front of them. The boat began sneakily slinking back around towards Half-Land, but he convinced it otherwise with a sharp pull on an oar.

"Your boat has other ideas, perhaps," Marietta shouted, smiling.

"Aye, she's stubborn as the witch that cursed her, this one. But she'll get us there, no worries, in her own time."

"The witch that cursed her?"

"Aye," said the man, nodding at the Island almost lost in the mist ahead, "she's really a horse, you see. Terrified of water she was, and she once nearly trampled a witch to get away from a waterfall. She didn't mean any harm," he said, fondly rubbing one side of the boat, "but when she gets scittery, she can be a mite dangerous. The witch cursed her so she'd have to spend her days in water. Turned her into a boat right under me, she did," he said, now rubbing a sore memory on his bottom.

"I came down with such a mighty thump that I turned into a boatkeeper, and a boatkeeper I've been, ever since." He smiled, but sadness tugged at one end of the smile, pulling it a bit lopsided.

"What were you before?"

"A mounted lamp-keeper," he answered, pulling himself up a bit straighter. "I held a lamp in the Queen of Half Land's processions to light her way from the castle to the keep. I was one of the better ones, though I shouldn't say so. Finest work in all Incunabula." He sighed. Marietta could have sworn the boat sighed with him, but perhaps it was the Shadowlark cradled in her pocket or a spare breeze crossing the top of an oar.

"Never mind, never mind," said the boatkeeper, pulling briskly on one oar as if it were a rein. "I promised to take care of her when she were nought but a tangle-legged colt, and I mean to keep my promise."

"Can't the witch change her back?"

"Reckon she could, if she could be found, but I won't leave Nellie in other hands, and no one'll search on our behalf."

"I will," said Marietta, "if you'll tell me who she is."

"She's the Mistress of the Tides," said the man, "or, leastways she *was*. The last anyone heard of her, she was heading into the Land of Infinite Variations. She could be anything by now. But if you can find her," said the boatkeeper, one hand rubbing the top of the oar as if to comfort it, "and get her to change her mind, well, we'd be grateful, no mistake."

Marietta nodded, and they continued to Tumble Island in silence.

When they reached the Island and the horse-boat bumped gently against the dock, Marietta reached out a cold hand and gently stroked the edge of the boat. For a moment, she could feel the soft coat, the powerful muscles, the steaming heat of the horse beneath.

"Soon, when you're a horse again," Marietta whispered, "I'll bring you an apple."

The little boat rocked gently under her hand, and she knew that Nellie understood. The boatkeeper would accept no pay, but he urged them to be quick in their business or they'd be stuck on the Island for the long winter season.

"I can't put Nellie at the risk of the waves," he said, and Marietta liked him even better for it. He gave them directions to the home of the Storyteller, and they headed off for the far side of Tumble Island.

After about ten steps, Marietta understood why the wizard fell down so much. Tumble Island *moved*. It rocked and leaned with the waves, exactly as a boat would. After growing up here, it would be very difficult to learn balance on land that stood still. Marietta fell down several times until she learned the special stumbling, halting step the movement of the Island required.

Deep inside her pocket, Shadowlark groaned. "If I'd wanted waves, I'd have been born a duck. This is worse than that galloping boat!"

Marietta laughed. "Sorry, Shadowlark," she said. "I'll try to be quick getting there and back. Meanwhile, what does the wizard's notebook say about the Trolls of Tumble Island?"

"It's too dark in here to read," grumbled the Shadowlark, "and too bouncing-and-leaning by half." But a moment later, Marietta heard the muffled sound of pages being turned.

The Trolls of Questionable Origin are one of the great mysteries of Incunabula. Brutish, nasty and short, their greatest pleasure is in playing mean tricks and not getting caught. They kick chairs from beneath innocent bottoms, are expert at leaping unexpectedly from dark places, and they can say 'nyah nyah nyah' in one hundred and eleven Incunabulan languages. No one knows where they came from, or they'd surely have been sent back there by now. The only way to defeat a Troll is to tickle it helpless, but the Trolls know this and have developed an effective defense: they never wash. Their smell is so horrible that no one can get close enough to tickle them. The advantage of this is, of course, that from downwind, you know they're coming long before they reach you. If they catch you outside, lie down quickly and make a snow angel around you. The Trolls will leave you alone if you do. If they catch you inside, you must teach them a new trick before they'll let you go. (Be aware that they'll use your trick on others, so try not to make it too nasty.) Fortunately, the Trolls are extremely stupid. As the Duchess of Popcorn once said, 'If they stood still long enough, someone would probably build a barn out of them.'

"That's all there is," said the Shadowlark. "None too helpful, really, and the wizard's handwriting is appalling. Still, any information may prove useful." The bird's head suddenly popped out of Marietta's pocket. "Are we there yet?"

"We've only just started, Shadowlark," Marietta answered. "We've got a long way to go, and the snow is so deep it slows me down."

"Hmph," grumbled the bird, snuggling back into the soft warmth of the coat pocket, "doesn't look that deep to *me*. Really, why choose legs when you could have wings, I ask myself?" The bird's head popped out again. "Marietta, keep an eye out for purple berries, will you? All this traveling makes me terribly hungry."

"Of course," said Marietta, and she smiled to herself.

Marietta slogged on in snow that was sometimes only over the tops of her shoes, but more often just under her knees. It was very hard work, walking this way, and it took all her breath; she was glad that Shadowlark wasn't in the mood for conversation. As she headed down the road to the Apex Pagoda, far away on the windward side of Tumble Island, Marietta came upon a man crawling on his hands and knees, scrabbling in the snow.

"I've lost it!" he shouted to the sky. "I've lost it," he murmured to the road. "I've lost it and soon I will die."

"What have you lost?" asked Marietta, for she was always a very helpful girl.

"My heart! I've lost my heart! It slipped from my pocket and fell into the snow, and I cannot live without my heart until the thaw begins."

"I'll help you find it," said Marietta, who really was terribly helpful, and she knelt down on the road and buried her hands in the snow. "Is it very big?"

"Oh, no" said the man, "but it's very pretty and shiny and swings on the end of a silver chain, and it counts the seconds of my life, and oh, what a short life it will be . . . . " The man began to weep, and he lay down in the snow.

Marietta searched and searched until her hands were purple and she was tired, and then she too lay down in the snow. She made a quick snow angel around her to protect her from the Trolls of Questionable Origin, and for a little while, she slept. When she awoke, she heard a ticking noise, rather like the ticking of clockwork beetles. She reached her hand into the snow beside her ear, and she felt something very cold and hard just beside her head. She pulled it from the snow. It was a pocketwatch on a silver chain.

"My heart! You've found my heart!" came a voice from behind her head. The man took the watch from Marietta's hand, unzipped his chest, and slipped the watch inside. His face, which was pale and white, quickly grew rosy, and his smile was wide enough for three ordinary smiles. "For this I must reward you," said the man, and from his pocket he pulled a small dictionary. "I notice you are a very quiet girl," said the man, "and I wonder if perhaps you do not have enough words. So I give you this reward: in here are all the words of all the languages in all the world. For life has many questions, and you should never be without a ready answer."

He handed Marietta the dictionary and then skipped off down the road, spraying snow in all directions. Marietta slipped the dictionary deep into a pocket and continued on to find the Storyteller in the Apex Pagoda, far away on the windward side of Tumble Island.

Chapter Nine

In an effort to break up the seemingly endless trudge to the Apex Pagoda, Marietta spoke to the bird in her pocket. "Shadowlark," she said, "what was your life like before we met?"

Shadowlark had somehow managed to find purple berries in this frozen place, and steady crunching had come from her pocket for the past hour, along with frequent seeds.

"I imagine that's your Earth way of asking the color of my life?"

"Color?"

"Mmmm." Shadowlark's head emerged from the pocket. He blinked several times in the bright sunlight. "Where I come from, lives are described a bit differently. You, for example, might say your life is 'good' or 'happy.' I, on the other hand, would tell you that my life is yellow with bits of green and blue, is rounded at the corners and smooth to the touch. It's much the same, you see?"

"Actually, I *do* see," said Marietta, who was astonished to find she did. "My life tastes like raspberries, and it's so light it floats. It's mostly white with bits of pink and blue around the edges. Sometimes it's so tall, I can't see the top of it."

"That's because you're very young," said the Shadowlark, nodding. "It's just as it should be."

"Shadowlark," Marietta began, a little hesitantly, "do you like traveling with me?"

"Your shoulder is just the right width for my claws," the bird answered, "and your coat pocket just the right depth. You happily stop to pick berries when we find them, and your hair is the perfect shield when the light is too strong. Being carried is nothing like flying, of course, but at least your shoulder is a comfortable distance from the ground."

"Ah," said Marietta, who felt that perhaps that wasn't quite the answer she was looking for. "I see."

"But it's rather more than that," the bird continued, as if Marietta hadn't spoken. "Where I come from, we have a saying: 'You catch the beat of my wings.'" He crunched hard on some berries and fell silent.

"What does that mean, exactly?" Marietta asked.

"It means that you understand me, we are in rhythm," said the bird, in a soft voice. "And, together, we fly." He was quiet again for a long moment. "That should make you happy, stuck on the ground as you are." He snickered quietly in her ear.

Marietta smiled to herself, her heart full of bursting, golden bubbles that warmed her through. "The ground's not so bad," she replied, "not when you have a friend to travel it with."

And the snow began to fall again.

"Marietta?" asked Shadowlark, some time later, "do you smell something . . . awful?"

"Trolls," said Marietta. "That's got to be trolls." The smell was strong enough to flip her stomach like a pancake on a griddle. It was old onions and green slimy things at the back of the refrigerator with a hint of dirty socks and the goop at the bottom of the kitchen garbage can.

"What do you suggest we do?" asked the bird. "Besides holding our breath, that is."

"Run and hide?" asked Marietta, wiping her watering eyes.

"I expected something more heroic," said the bird, "but perhaps *run and hide* is best."

They ran, but it was very difficult to find a place to hide in this frozen landscape. There were few trees, and their branches were so bare that they would provide no cover. There were some large rocks, so Marietta headed for those, Shadowlark bouncing rather violently in her pocket as she ran. They tucked themselves among the rocks and peered around to watch for the trolls. Even there, way back between high boulders, the smell was overpowering.

Only moments later, there was a rumble like a hundred galloping horses, and the trolls burst out from behind some boulders, a very short distance from where Marietta and Shadowlark were hiding. The trolls were about Marietta's height, but thickly built. You could set a full plate of food on each of a troll's shoulders (which I wouldn't suggest doing, really, but you *could*, and anyway a whiff of a troll can take away your appetite for days), set him off running (never a bad thing, provided he's running *away*), and the plates will never fall. He could run until the food smelled as bad as he did, but the plates would never fall, never break, so broad were his shoulders.

They had short, wiry green hair and thick, stubby fingers, and though Marietta had never seen anything like them before, somehow they looked oddly familiar. They were all standing in a circle, facing out, and sniffing the air like dogs searching for a scent.

"They'll never find us that way, don't worry," came the sandpaper voice of the Shadowlark in Marietta's ear. "How could they when they all stink to the moon?"

Marietta didn't answer. She wanted to get closer, to take a better look at their faces. From here, they all appeared to be identical. Suddenly one troll sniffed hard, pulling in so much air that his chest expanded even more, buttons popping in a row off his shirt front. He turned to look precisely in their direction, and Marietta gasped.

"It's OK," said Shadowlark, smoothing her hair with one raggedy wing. "He can't see us." The little bird was astonished to find that Marietta was laughing.

"Oh no! Oh no" she kept saying, tears of laughter running down her face. She was trying hard not to make any noise, but now and again a strangled laugh would bubble up to the top of her throat and escape.

"What can possibly be so funny?" asked the Shadowlark, wings on his hips. "Really, Marietta, this is not the proper response to a life-and-death situation, particularly when the life in question is *mine.*"

"I'm sorry!" Marietta managed to squeeze the words from her laughed-out lungs which were surely the size of raisins by now. "It's those *trolls!*"

"Shhhhhh! I depend on you to save me, but I doubt very much if you can if you're just a wet heap of giggles."

Marietta took a deep breath (which she immediately regretted, as the smell of the trolls could stagger the noseless Minister of Satisfying Sneezes), and tried to get her laughter under control. She was attacked by a few lingering giggles, but little by little, she calmed down.

"It's all right, Shadowlark," said Marietta. "I know those trolls. I made them."

"What?!" The bird nearly tumbled off her shoulder in surprise.

Marietta nodded. "I'd forgotten about them. Look at their faces — each one could be the twin brother of Billy-down-the-block! Apart from the green hair, that is. Billy used to pick on me all the time and pull my braids and call me names, so I turned him into a troll in my imagination. But why are there so many of them?"

Marietta didn't know that birds could snort, but obviously this one could. First one snort, then a pair of them, then a whole chain of snorts rattled from the bird's beak. It took Marietta a moment to realize that Shadowlark was laughing. He laughed and he snickered and he snorted and chortled; he might have even guffawed at one point, but Marietta couldn't be sure. She stood and waited patiently for him to stop as he had waited for her a moment ago, and she wondered when was the last time anyone had gotten so much laughter from the Trolls of Questionable Origin?

"Oh, Marietta, what if all children of Earth were like you?" he whistled at last, snickering and wiping his eyes with one feather. "You could have given us wondrous creatures with that fine imagination of yours, and instead you plague us with some of the nastiest, smelliest, most unpleasant beasts in all of Incunabula. Some hero!"

One of Shadowlark's giggles had apparently lodged in Marietta's throat, and now it wiggled out as only giggles can wiggle when you're trying to giggle quietly or not at all. "I didn't know my troll would become real somewhere else! But it isn't *all* my fault — I didn't make him smelly."

"Oh dear, never mind. How many of them are there? I count thirteen."

"Thirteen," Marietta agreed. "Thirteen Billy-down-the-blocks."

"Fourteen," said a voice from a rock above them, making them both jump in surprise. "Thirteen plus one makes fourteen. Thirteen to stand in a circle and smell, and one to hunt and catch. You come with me, bird and girl."

It was another troll. His big, horrible, greasy face was just above them, but because the wind blew between the rocks and not from top-to-bottom, they couldn't smell him. Marietta peered out from the rocks to see if they might possibly escape, but they were surrounded now. They'd spent so much time giggling they'd forgotten to keep a watch on what the trolls were doing.

"I am *not* going to tell Billy about this," Marietta muttered to herself. "Some hero."

As soon as Marietta emerged from the rocks, the trolls formed a sour-smelling circle around her. They did look like Billy-down-the-block, but only sort of. Obviously those creatures that were born in an Earth child's imagination and came to live here continued to grow and change even after the child had forgotten them. Marietta felt a bit guilty about making Billy into one of these nasty trolls – he wasn't so bad, really; certainly not as bad as *this*.

The fourteen trolls stood and stared and said nothing.

"Shadowlark," Marietta whispered to the bird under her hair, "can I still control them, if I made them?"

"I don't know," rasped the bird in her ear. "Why not try?"

So Marietta imagined the trolls suddenly deciding to be good and kind and to wash every day, but nothing happened except that the troll circle drew tighter around them, and that was a very bad thing indeed.

"Is this what you imagined?" asked Shadowlark, his eyes streaming.

"Don't be ridiculous," whispered Marietta, wrinkling her nose halfway up her forehead. "Why would I want these horrible creatures closer to me?"

"Do you want us to teach you a trick?" Shadowlark asked the trolls, looking around the ring for a possible leader.

"No. Hold you for the Prince," one answered.

"He teaches better tricks than girl," said another.

This was bad. The trolls were in league with the Dark Prince. They squeezed together even more, shrinking the circle further.

"Stay in circle til Prince come."

"Shadowlark, we've got to get away from them," whispered Marietta. "And quickly. We don't have much time."

"I'd love nothing better. What do you suggest?"

Suddenly the troll smell was *much* stronger, and Marietta nearly screamed when a great, greasy paw settled on her shoulder. A troll was behind her, holding something out to her with the other hand. It was a mirror. The troll gestured again that Marietta should take it, so she did, stifling a "thank you" that nearly popped out. The troll moved back to his place in the great, smelly circle.

As she studied the mirror, the glass began to move, swirling and twisting and writhing before shaping itself into the face of the Dark Prince. Startled, Marietta dropped the mirror into the snow and left it there. She couldn't see the Prince's face under the snow, but she could hear his horrible voice.

"Pick me up," he said, his voice sharp as knives and pointed as tacks.

"No," said Marietta, angry to hear her voice shaking. "I don't have to."

"Pick up the mirror, Marietta."

"No. If you have something to say, then say it. But I don't have to look at your ugly face."

"Oh for crying out- *look*, you're only making things worse for yourself."

"Funny, I thought not looking at you was making things better."

"I've given these trolls orders to stay in this circle until the winds come. You'll be trapped on Tumble Island until spring, and by then Incunabula will be mine. I've closed all the doors, Marietta. When Incunabula reaches the end of its magic supply, it will die, and all its inhabitants with it. Even the Moon Shadow Tigers. And the Shadowlark. Even you, Earth girl. Have you ever seen something starve to death? It's terribly cruel and painful. This place will shrivel and slowly digest itself until nothing is left. How awfully, awfully sad." And the Prince started to laugh. The heat of his hatred was melting the snow around the mirror, and now the Prince's face was plain to see.

"Why are you doing this? Who are you and what has Incunabula done to you to make you hate it so much?"

The Prince's smile disappeared, replaced with a look much more grim. "Never mind. My reasons are not for you to know. The trolls are instructed to stand in this circle until spring, so there's no way for you to get food or water or warmth. So you and that stupid bird will be the first to experience death by starvation. Perhaps you should take notes."

Marietta had heard enough. She lifted her right foot and brought it down hard on the mirror, her new shoes grinding the glass to dust.

"Fly away, Shadowlark," said Marietta. "You can fly where they can't reach you."

"Don't be ridiculous, Marietta," said the bird. "I have a pocket full of purple berries and complete confidence in you." He settled himself back into her pocket and hummed a bit before falling asleep. Things were very quiet for a long while as Marietta thought and the trolls . . . didn't.

"Troll," said Marietta, to the one who had handed her the mirror (or at least she thought it was the same one), "what exactly are your instructions? To stand in this circle? Whether or not the bird and I are in it?"

"Stand in circle 'til spring," answered the troll. "Don't move for anything."

"Excellent," said Marietta. Holding her breath so tightly it squeaked, she ran directly toward the ring of trolls. They were squished together so tightly that the trolls were knee-to-knee and shoulder-to-shoulder. Marietta was just able to fit her foot in the space between the knees and the space between the shoulders and climb up the trolls. She launched herself off a troll head and was running before she hit the ground on the other side.

Just as she'd suspected, the trolls didn't move. When she got a safe distance away, she turned back to look. The trolls were obviously concerned and agitated, not knowing what to do. Their orders were to stand in a circle until spring, and they were relatively sure Marietta was supposed to be trapped in the middle. But they had their orders, and so they stayed, squeezed in their noxious circle, until spring.

In fact, no one knows what happened to them after that. There is a ring of fourteen stones – in approximately the place where Marietta was held – that some believe is the trolls, frozen in indecision and confusion, forever. In any case, the Trolls of Questionable Origin were neither seen nor smelt again after they met Marietta, and no one has missed them a bit.

The Apex Pagoda was at the top of the tallest mountain of Tumble Island, and it took Marietta many more days of slogging through deep snow to reach it. The Storyteller, like the Rainbow Maker, didn't much care for guests, and so he built his house in the most distant and isolated place on the Island. It was terribly windy at the top of the mountain, and his house was built so high that no trees grew there. The place had an icy beauty to it, but it was not a friendly place, not a welcoming place at all. Marietta found herself shivering when she finally reached the Apex Pagoda, and not all of her shivering was caused by the cold wind that blew through her coat and then through her bones.

The Apex Pagoda was actually a very simple wooden cabin, small and humble. It didn't look big enough to hold all the stories that had ever been told, but then many things in Incunabula were different than they seemed, and Marietta was getting used to surprises.

The cabin stood on stilts, one at each corner. The stilts were driven far down into the ice cap that formed the top of the mountain and which never melted, no matter how hot the sun shone on it. The cabin might sink an inch or two in the summer as the top layers of ice retreated below it, but when winter came, the ice re-formed, and raised the cabin back again.

To get into the Storyteller's house, Marietta had to climb up one of the stilts which had posts driven into it to provide hand- and foot-holds. It was not the easiest or cleanest or most comfortable way to enter someone's house, but then the Storyteller wasn't much concerned if his guests were comfortable.

At the top of the stilt was a trapdoor which led into the Pagoda. Marietta, her hands nearly frozen, thumped on the door above her head, and was very relieved when it opened, almost immediately. She climbed up inside the cabin, and the shock of warmth nearly took her breath away.

"You may be too late," rattled a voice near her, a voice that sounded like a wooden box full of rusty nails being shaken. "The Creeping Nasties have been devouring my library, and perhaps the story you need is already gone. Come."

Marietta's eyes had only just gotten used to the dimness inside the cabin. It was warm, and there was a fire, but the fire seemed to light only an inch or two in front of it, and the rest of the cabin fell into darkness. Shadowlark immediately flew down to stand in front of the fire, partially to warm himself, and partially to avoid too much darkness in this shadowy place. The Storyteller – Marietta assumed that was who that was – had shuffled off to another part of the cabin. Marietta stood for a moment, warming her hands in front of the strangely dim fire, before following the bent back that was all she had so far seen of the Storyteller.

The Apex Pagoda was definitely bigger on the inside than the outside, for they entered a room so huge and thickly packed with books that Marietta could hardly see to the far end of it.

"Listen!" said the Storyteller, turning suddenly to face Marietta. "Can you hear the sound of chewing? That is the Creeping Nasties, eating my wonderful stories of musical dragons and captured princes and leaving nothing but their bones. Beautiful tales of heroic rescues are becoming stories about mold growing on stones; happy endings are turning tragic." He pointed a long, crooked finger at Marietta. "Work quickly, Earthchild; time is running out."

The Storyteller was small inside his dark, dusty cloak. He was bent and wore thick glasses, his eyes watery behind the fat lenses. Thin, gray hair fell down his shoulders and back, and his voice was so rattling and creaking, it was hard to hear his words under all that noise. But his narrow, dark brown eyes were quietly kind, and Marietta quickly got over her fear of this strange little man shaped like a question mark.

"I . . . I don't know where to start," Marietta stammered, looking down the vast rows of shelves, each crammed so tightly with books that there wasn't even room for a bookworm to crawl between the pages. "I'm not really sure what I'm looking for."

The Storyteller disappeared behind a teetering stack of books and came back a moment later with two short stools. He set these on the floor and sat on the taller one. "Sit down, Marietta, and I'll tell you the story of another Earth hero who came to save this land."

Marietta and the Creeping Nasties

Marietta sat on the short, rickety stool in that long, dark room full of books and listened to the bent little man whose voice had suddenly turned from rusty nails rattling in a tin can to chocolate cream and silk.

"The man in the amazing icicle suit [the Storyteller began] was responsible for cleaning the cages of the frost dragons and the snow leopards and keeping them well fed with marshmallows and peppermint tea. They stayed in their cages, the leopards and the dragons, until the end of autumn was officially announced by the Queen. Then the leopards were freed to shed snow from their fur as they ran from one end of the kingdom to the other, and the dragons were released to freeze the lakes and blow patterns of frost on the windows.

"All winter the leopards and the dragons would prowl, and the people would hear their snarling in the icy wind that wrapped around their faces and scuttled down their backs no matter how tightly they wrapped their scarves and buttoned their collars. They did their jobs very well, the leopards and the dragons, for the snow covered the land thickly, muffling the sounds of spring underneath. And the lakes were frozen so completely, that if the world were turned upside-down, the lakes would slide out whole in solid chunks like ice cubes from an ice cube tray.

"And when the world was so cold outside, it was necessary to warm from within, so the people sat down together at one long table, so long that it stretched from one end of the room to the other and around the corner and back again. And the table was loaded with food: jeweled potatoes, baked in their golden crusts; long, thin carrot fingers with rings at the thicker end; tart cranberry soups and sweet blackberry puddings; pears studded with raisins, and apples stuffed with sweet breads and cinnamon; wispy tendrils of angel's hair grass floated in rich sauces. And the more the people ate, the warmer and the jollier they became. They toasted each other's health and long life, and together they gave thanks for the snow leopards and the frost dragons who provided such a splendid excuse for feasting and fellowship.

"But one year, the snow leopards and the frost dragons refused to come back to their cages when winter was over, and the land stayed locked in the cold and the ice for many months past the official end of the season. The Queen searched far and wide for a hero who could control the winter-bringing creatures, but there was no such hero to be found in all of Incunabula. Finally, the Queen agreed to send to Earth for the hero this land required.

"The Earth hero's name was Max, and Max was a good, gentle and obedient boy. He seemed an unlikely champion, for he was so small and frail compared to the might of the dragons and the leopards, but Max had the warmest heart in all the world. His heart was so warm, you could feel the heat when he passed you by, and with his good and kind heart he melted the ice and brought the trees into bud.

"The snow leopards and the frost dragons bent their knees to him, and Max gently led them back to their cages to spend the spring and summer in sleep. But all this cold and frost had planted a tiny sliver of Incunabulan ice in Max's heart.

"As the ice spread and thickened inside Max, so he became colder and harder. He was not able to go home to Earth with his heart encased in Incunabulan ice, so he took to roaming the land, spreading bitterness and chill where once he had spread sunlight and springtime. This hero of Incunabula became its greatest enemy. He was no longer able to grow up, for the ice had frozen his body; he was no longer able to be kind, for the ice had frozen his heart. To warm himself, he turned to hate, and the heat of his anger and loathing burned a scowl on his face and scarred his heart forever. One day, he simply disappeared into the depths of the Great Cratered Cobweb, never to be seen again. And that is the story of Max."

When the tale was told, the Storyteller fell into silence the way you or I might fall into a deep hole: suddenly and completely. Marietta sat for a moment, waiting for him to continue or perhaps to explain why he'd told her this story, but he said nothing more. His dark brown eyes watched her closely from under the hood of his cloak, but he remained silent and offered no explanation.

"I'm not sure I understand," said Marietta. "What does this have to do with the Dark Prince of Dullardry? Unless . . . " she began, suddenly struck by a thought, "you think that Max *became* the Dark Prince? Is it possible that Max is still alive? The wizard told me that this other hero was here many thousands of years ago."

"Many things are possible for Earth children who come to Incunabula," said the Storyteller, and his voice was once again a drawer full of old scissors and dull, rusty knives. "And time is different here."

"I remember once the Dark Prince *flickered*," said Marietta, searching back in her memory the way the Storyteller might search through his shelves full of books, "He seemed uncertain for a moment, and he flickered, and I could see there was something else behind. As if he wasn't really real, almost."

"Somewhere in these shelves there is more of his story, Marietta; more that you should know if you are to fight him and win."

"But there are millions of books here!" Marietta cried, and her voice ran down the aisles, shaking loose some of the dust as it bounced from side to side. "I'll never find the right story in time. And what if it's already gone?"

"You must sacrifice your orange bead," said the Storyteller, standing up from his stool. "If the story remains on the shelves, the light of the orange bead will find it. Be quick, child of Earth. The disease spreads faster every day, and no one knows if Max's fate may be your fate as well." And he shuffled out of the library and back towards the fire.

The Storyteller's last words sent a chill of fear up Marietta's back, a chill that ran up and down her spine a few times before coming to rest in her stomach. With both hands, she pushed his words aside, and pulled the string of rainbow beads from her neck. The tigers had told her to hold on to the beads, but there seemed to be no other way to find the story she needed. The red one had already gone to save the Shadowlark from the spirit gum mine. With the orange one gone to find the story, she'd have only five beads left. With trembling fingers, she pulled the orange bead free from the string, and held it up in the air.

"Find the story," she whispered to the bright glass ball, "show me where to read what I need to know."

The little orange bead began to glow, faintly at first, and then brighter and brighter. It slowly lifted up from the tips of Marietta's fingers, and then floated down one of the many aisles of books in the library. It moved from side to side and from book to book as if searching the titles. It flew slowly at first, and Marietta was able to follow it, but soon its movement became fast and frantic. The little light zipped and flashed through the library: now here, now over there, a streak of light above her head. Finally, it came to rest on a single book, and the brightness of its glow increased to lead Marietta to the shelf where the book lay.

As soon as Marietta had the book in her hand, the light began to fade, finally dying away completely, and the little orange bead disappeared with a quiet pop no louder than the pop of a soap bubble. Marietta took the book back to her stool, opened it up and began to read.

Chapter Ten

The library was cold and growing colder every minute, but Marietta didn't even notice. Shadowlark was asleep on a thick pillow in front of the fireplace, and the hours burned away and crumbled to dust, just as the logs in the fire did. Still Marietta read and read and read the story of Max, a little boy from Earth who had come to save Incunabula but who was now perhaps the greatest threat Incunabula had ever faced. The more Marietta read, the more she was convinced that Max was behind the Dark Prince, and that was why the Dark Prince was *different*, not subject to Incunabulan laws.

Like Marietta, Max had been brought to Incunabula from a small town on Earth. The earliest stories described Max as a wonderful boy with laughter like golden bells and a heart big enough and brave enough to save a world. But somehow he had been pierced by Incunabulan ice, and that ice had changed everything. According to several of the later stories, Max was seen from time to time in the Bleaklands, an area of darkness just on the other side of the Illuminated Village. But Max had disappeared entirely many hundreds of years ago, blending into the darkness, and finally becoming nothing more than a distant, unhappy memory, a dark blot on the pages of Incunabulan history books.

"I don't understand how such a nice boy can become so bad," Marietta murmured to herself, closing the book at last. "Why couldn't the warmth of his heart melt the ice instead of the cold ice freezing him?"

"An excellent question," said the Storyteller, emerging suddenly from the dangling shadows and startling Marietta. "And one that no one has ever been able to answer."

"Most of my questions turn out that way," said Marietta, sighing a little and straightening her tired back. "I guess I'm off to the Bleaklands next. That's where he was last seen, so that's where I'll start." Marietta stood up and stretched a bit more, unknotting her arms and legs.

"You can't leave until the Apex Pagoda has regained its balance." The Storyteller's face looked grim and serious beneath his hood, and even his eyes no longer seemed so kind.

"What does that mean? I have to return to Half-Land quickly before the winter winds come."

"My home is very carefully balanced on four stilts driven deep into the ice. If that balance is upset, then the Pagoda will fall. You take away a story with you; this upsets the delicate balance upon which my home depends."

"So what can I do?"

"You must leave a story behind. It's the only way."

"How do I do that?"

"You sit on that stool, and I sit on this one, and you give me a story to leave behind you."

"Oh, I'm really not a good storyteller," said Marietta, pulling up the tall stool, but not sitting on it. "I mean, I'm not very good with words, generally; that is, actually I tell stories all the time, really, but to little kids, and *you're* a storyteller, after all, and I'd feel silly trying to tell a story to *you*, and, oh gosh, isn't there some other way?"

It was difficult to tell, since the Storyteller's hood covered so much of his face, but Marietta thought perhaps the kindness had come back to his eyes, and there might just be the tiniest crease of a smile running across his lips.

Telling a story to a storyteller takes a special kind of courage, rather like making a sandwich for a great chef or sending an opera singer to sleep with a lullaby. Marietta felt terribly foolish as she perched awkwardly on the taller of the two stools and took a deep breath to begin.

"Once upon a time-" she started.

"Which time?" asked the Storyteller. "And who is standing on it and how?"

"I'm sorry?" asked Marietta, confused. "I don't understand."

"Well, *that's* a fine beginning, if even the teller doesn't understand the story," grumbled the bent old man. "Try again, but stick to what you know, if you please."

"But that's how stories begin," Marietta protested. "They always have, that's all. It doesn't *mean* anything."

The Storyteller leaned forward, so close that his long, sharp nose would have popped Marietta's bubble-gum bubble, had there been one to pop.

"Stories must always mean something," the Storyteller said, his voice low and deep and serious. "For here in Incunabula, as a story is told, so is it written, somewhere in the vast darkness of my shelves. As you talk, you will hear the quiet scribbling of your story being recorded, copied into the history of this place." The Storyteller leaned back on his stool and crossed his arms. "Therefore I ask that you please keep nonsense to a minimum. I haven't room to waste on meaningless gibberish."

Marietta opened her mouth to begin again, but every word died on her tongue or was swallowed back again, having failed to pass the gibberish test. She hadn't realized how much nonsense she carried around in her brain and resolved to clear it out as soon as she had the time. Meanwhile, she had a story to tell, and she could hear, just outside the Storyteller's windows, a few scraps of the first winter winds chasing one another around the Apex Pagoda and down the mountainside. She and Shadowlark had to leave Tumble Island, and soon. Marietta slipped one cold hand into her pocket to warm it, and there she found the dictionary given to her by the man with his heart on a silver chain. The minute her hand touched the book, her mind became filled with words, wonderful, shining words that cascaded and tumbled around in her brain like the precious stones in the Great Jeweled Falls of Fought-About River.

"Do you know about the Flightless Beetles?" she asked the Storyteller, and she sat a bit taller on her stool.

"No," he answered, a smile tugging at his lips like a very small child tugging on the collar of a very large dog.

"Very well, then, I'll tell you about the Flightless Beetles, but you must sit very still and not interrupt," [Marietta said this because she knew that's how all stories *really* begin – and they do, don't they?] "The tiny flightless beetles are born at the foot of Beetle-Trudge Peak, one of the tallest mountains in all of Incunabula. They spend their entire lives climbing the mountain, their tiny beetle feet covering only inches of mountain a day on a mountain that stretches upward for miles. It takes them many years to climb to the very top of Beetle-Trudge Peak, and they are always in danger of being snatched off the mountain by the beetle-eating birds or gobbled up whole by beetle-greedy snakes.

"But the Flightless Beetles have a secret: all along their path up the mountain side, with every tiny step they take, *wings* slowly grow underneath their hard beetle shells. These are not ordinary wings; these are glowing, multicolored beetle wings, wings of swirled colors that are always changing and never still. And those beetles who reach the top of the mountain, those whose lives have been one great, weary trudge up the mountain side, when they arrive at the uppermost peak, they unfurl those marvelous wings in the thin mountain air and dry them in the sharp mountain sunlight, and they *fly*. They lean into the winds that spiral up the sides of Beetle-Trudge Peak, and for a few short moments, they are the most wondrous, most beautiful, most spectacular creatures that ever lived.

"When, after their breath-stopping flight, they reach the bottom of Beetle-Trudge Mountain, they lose their glorious wings, and shortly

96

thereafter, they die. Some people think the beetles are very foolish, spending the whole of their lives clambering up the side of a mountain in exchange for one short tumble down it, when instead they could choose to live long, meaningful lives on the plains, and never grow wings at all. But the beetles refuse to listen to those who would persuade them to give up their wings, and generation after generation of Flightless Beetles turn their heads and feet towards the mountain as soon as they are born.

"I once asked a flightless beetle if he would trade his life for another, now that his flight was done and his wings gone and his life sputtering and flickering at the end of its wick.

" 'One life,' replied the beetle, 'is such a small price to pay for a moment or two of glorious Flight.' "

When Marietta had finished her story, she waited in silence for the Storyteller's response. He was very quiet for a long moment, his face almost entirely hidden in the darkness of his hood. Only the tip of his nose was visible, so Marietta looked at it, but as silent seconds stretched into minutes, Marietta realized how very little of interest there is in the tip of someone's nose. She cleared her throat and readjusted herself on her stool, wondering if perhaps her story had sent the old man to sleep. She stared at the nose some more, trying to get up the courage to shake the old man's knee when the Shadowlark called loudly to them from the other room.

"Marietta, the winds are growing!" he called, his voice shattering the silence into a thousand pieces. He couldn't come in to the library for fear of its overwhelming darkness, so he stood in the doorway, cupped his wings to his mouth, and shouted again. "We must go, and quickly!"

"I know, Shadowlark," Marietta called back, more quietly. "We're nearly ready to go."

The Storyteller pushed his hood back slightly from his face, and his eyes were kindly again as they looked into Marietta's.

"Your story is welcome here," he told her. "And one dark night I will find it again, and read it, and remember. Now go. Save as many of my tales as you can from Incunabula's disease."

Marietta nodded and stood, suddenly desperate with the need to move as fast as she could back to the boat and away from the Island, to wherever the Dark Prince was hiding. She was out the trapdoor and down the stilt-ladder with Shadowlark in her pocket before her stool had stopped rocking on its uncertain legs. The Storyteller was glad for her haste. As he stood in the cold darkness of his library, he could hear the quiet crunching of his stories being devoured by the Creeping Nasties, and he wished Marietta all necessary speed.

The journey down the mountain from the Apex Pagoda was rather faster than the slow trudge up. Shadowlark simply flew to the bottom, and Marietta, after tucking her hair into her coat, curled tightly into a ball and *rolled*. At the bottom of the mountain, the giant snowball with Marietta inside it hit a tree and exploded, leaving her dizzy but unhurt. She quickly got to her feet again, tucked Shadowlark into the deep, warm pocket he favored, and ran as fast as she could for the docks on the other side of Tumble Island.

They had no adventures on this trip, although adventures beckoned from every corner and beneath every rock. There were no run-ins with Trolls (but Shadowlark kept his nose open for them, just in case), no strange little people searching for their hearts or any other internal organs, and in general their journey back to the docks was covered in slightly less than half the time. The boatkeeper and Nellie were waiting for them, and they left for Half-Land immediately. Because of the winds, the boatkeeper and his horse-boat would have to spend the winter in Half-Land, but they didn't mind. They had friends there, and Nellie was happy to be away from Tumble Island whose rocking reminded her of water.

"Did you find what you needed to know, then?" asked the boatkeeper, once they were well under way.

"Yes. I think so." Marietta shivered and drew her coat closer around her as one of the winter winds tried to wrap itself around her neck and creep down her back. "Is Tumble Island always cold?"

"Aye," answered the boatkeeper, laughing, "cold and colder are the seasons we have here. Tumble Island has eleven warm days per year, and that's when everyone comes down with cold and flu."

"Do you actually *like* it here?" Marietta was mystified why anyone would stay in such an unfriendly place. Another freezing breeze tried to sneak in under the sleeve of her coat, but Marietta caught it and pulled it out by the tail.

"I do, aye," said the boatkeeper, smiling at Marietta, "for where the land is cold, the people are warm, and you'll not find any kinder people than those that live on Tumble Island. You'll have to come back and spend a winter here, when you've got the time. Feasts and music all season long. We look forward to our winters here," he said, winking at her, "for we've a good notion how to spend them."

"I'd like that," said Marietta, promising herself again that she'd find the witch who turned Nellie into a boat and force her to remove the curse. She had grown very fond of this kindly boatkeeper and his water-hating horse, and she wanted to help them. "A friend of mine is from Tumble Island."

"I believe I know that friend of yours," said the boatkeeper, grinning from ear to ear. "Something to do with explosions and love potions, I think." A movement in the sky caught his notice, and the boatkeeper looked up. "Mind your head now. You might want to put your hood up and your head down."

"What is it?" asked Marietta, straining to see what the boatkeeper saw.

"Umbrella bats," he answered. "Oddest thing. They come in great flocks, trying to catch children on their handles. They don't hurt them, though; just take them for the ride of their lives. Duck down now, quickly."

The sky darkened and then grew black as thousands and thousands of umbrella bats swarmed over them. The boatkeeper swung his oar at them, not to hurt them, just to scare them away. The boat rocked dangerously as he swiped at the sky, and Marietta feared they might overturn.

"They're a bit of a pain," he shouted, above the noise of thousands of wings, "still, we're glad of them. Incunabula hasn't had any new magic in quite some time, except these umbrella bats and a few other things here and there. So some imagination is getting through yet."

Umbrella bats. Marietta had told little Jenny about umbrella bats shortly before she came to Incunabula. Could these be hers? Or even Jenny's, maybe? Just as she was finishing this thought, the boat bumped gently against the dock of Half-Land, and their journey was over. Marietta climbed out of the boat, careful not to scrape the sides of the little craft with her shoes. She stroked Nellie for a moment, feeling again the soft horse-flesh waiting just under the wood.

"Can you point the way to the Bleaklands?" she asked the boatkeeper.

"I can," said the boatkeeper, his face creased with sudden concern, "but I'd rather not, if it's all the same to you. Why would you want to go to such a terrible place?"

"I think perhaps the Dark Prince is there," said Marietta. "I have to find him . . . and fight him."

"The Dark Prince of Dullardry? Is he behind all the nasty changes going on?"

"I think so. Please, I haven't much time. Which way to the Bleaklands?"

"A scrap of a girl like you, against a great wretched beast like him? Why, it's not a fair fight!"

"No, it isn't," said Marietta, a glint in her eye. "He'll need all the help he can get. Now, if you please, boatkeeper, the Bleaklands?"

Reluctantly, the boatkeeper pointed roughly westward, a route that led along the edge of the Divided Ocean before getting lost in the deep forests.

Marietta and the Creeping Nasties

"If I hadn't seen you with the Moon-Shadow Tigers, I'd come along with you," said the boatkeeper. "But I reckon you've got friends a mite more powerful than I am."

Marietta stood on tiptoe to kiss the boatkeeper on one cheek. Without another word, she headed off in the direction the boatkeeper had indicated.

It was warmer here than on Tumble Island, and Marietta was able to take off her heavy coat and stuff it into the special travelbag it had come in (first removing Shadowlark from the pocket, of course.) Although the thick forests and dreary Bleaklands were in front of her, Marietta felt quite content to walk in the sunshine along the banks of the Divided Ocean. Her sword thumped comfortably against her leg, both comforting her with its presence and reminding her that a time was coming when a sword might save her life. She strode on into the sunlit day, Shadowlark on her shoulder avoiding too much sunlight by wrapping her hair around him.

After a time, her route led away from the ocean and into the rolling hills beyond. It was very pleasant in the hills: fragrant flowers that had escaped the Creeping Nasties perfumed the air, birds sang cheerful greetings to Shadowlark who whistled back, stingless bees wove patterns in the air with their hums. It would have been a perfect afternoon if it hadn't been for the dragon who waited only fifty-six steps ahead.

Chapter Eleven

Fester and Ooze, the twin heads of the Ravenous Dragon of Gibbet Hill, had caught something and were preparing to make a meal of it when Marietta arrived. Marietta had met the Dragons once before, on Runaround Mountain, and she was friendly with Fester and Ooze, or at least as friendly as one can be with nasty, ugly dragon heads.

"What have you got there?" asked Marietta, but the Dragons would not answer, for they held their captive in their mouths and did not wish to drop him.

"Help! Oh, help an honest man who never hurt a soul in all his honest life!" It was Perfectly Frank who hung from the Dragons' mouths, the sleeve of his coat in Fester's mouth, and his trouser leg caught in Ooze's teeth. "Help before they tear me apart and feed on my virtuous bones!"

"Hello, Frank," said Marietta, looking up from below. "How nice to see you again, even from this angle."

"Marietta? Is that you?" cried Perfectly Frank, who now hung upside down, one trouser leg in each Dragon's mouth, his upside-down face staring directly into Marietta's rightside-up one.

"And how have you gotten into this mess?" asked Marietta, hoping the lie would be a good one.

"I . . . I . . . well," said Perfectly Frank, bouncing up and down in the air as the Dragons tore at his clothes, "I came this way to pick some herbs to heal a sick old lady who lives in yonder village, and these wretched Dragons leaped on me, and I was caught. I don't mind so much for myself, for to die horribly in an honest cause is all I ask of life," said Frank, who was now rightside-up but facing away from Marietta, so his voice was hard to hear. "But I do rather mind not being able to heal a sick old man who needed my aid."

"Woman," corrected Marietta. "It's a sick old *woman*. For the sake of the Moon, Frank, at least keep your stories straight."

"Woman, yes, woman!" cried Perfectly Frank, whose voice echoed terribly, now that his head was inside of Fester's mouth. "It is so difficult to remember such details when you expect to die at any moment, and those who could help you merely stand around making idle conversation."

"All right, all right," said Marietta, drawing her sword. "Fester, I know your head will grow back twice as powerful and uglier than ever, but do you really want the pain and inconvenience of having it chopped off in the first place? And Ooze, if I chop *your* head off, the mess that gushes forth from the stump will kill every living thing it touches for a hundred miles, and you'll have to go elsewhere to find food."

The Dragons immediately dropped Frank, choosing to find prey that tasted better and wiggled less and didn't come with the additional problem of causing one's head to be chopped off.

"He's a terrible liar," said Fester, nodding at Frank who lay on the ground, giggling, with his right thumb in his left ear. "He was being taken to the gallows to be executed. We made a deal with the Hangman because we prefer our food alive."

"That's right!" said Ooze. "He was going to be hanged for popping balloons and selling asparagus-flavored ice cream. They take their celebrations seriously around here, and to be a Party Pooper is a capital offense."

Marietta hauled Perfectly Frank to his feet, yanked his thumb out of his ear, and sent him on his way.

"Why did you let him go?" complained Ooze. "He would fill our belly for many days, and he's no use to the world."

"I don't know," said Marietta, watching Perfectly Frank knock over several little girls and steal their daisy chains as he made his way down the hill. "Perhaps someday he'll be useful to me. But for now," she said, waving her sword, "he is under my protection, and I don't want to find him in your mouths again." And she too headed off down Gibbet Hill, stopping briefly to weave a daisy chain a mile long and stronger than rope for the little girls.

Marietta and Shadowlark caught up with Frank at the bottom of Gibbet Hill; he had gotten the daisy chains caught around his legs and fallen over in a brightly-colored heap of flowers. He was struggling to free himself when Marietta found him.

"Frank, what are you doing?" Marietta asked, though the answer was perfectly obvious.

"Resting," said Frank, as he tore furiously at the blooms and stems (one-handed, as the other hand was stuck in his ear, of course).

Marietta leaned down to help untangle him, but the flower stems were strong, and Frank wouldn't hold still.

"Now you know why they call them daisy *chains*," said Shadowlark, flying in circles around Frank's head. "And this will teach you to steal flowers from little girls."

"I didn't steal them!" said Frank, indignantly. "They . . . those girls, they chased me down the hill and tied me up."

"They most certainly did not, Frank, and you know it," said Marietta. "Oh, hold still, and I'll cut the chains with my sword. Seems the only use it ever gets is in helping *you*."

A few whicks from the sword, and Frank was free, lying on the ground and surrounded by a confusion of tattered daisies and torn stems. Marietta helped Frank to his feet.

"Such violence was unnecessary," humphed Frank, dusting daisy petals from his coat. "I could have freed myself easily, only I didn't want to destroy the lovely flowers."

"Hmmmm. I suppose 'thank you' is too much to ask," said Marietta, pulling a daisy stem from behind Frank's left ear.

"Not at all! And you're very welcome, don't mention it." And Frank started off down the road toward the Bleaklands.

"Where are you headed?" Marietta called after him, knowing the question was pointless. Frank didn't answer, only kept walking, fast, along the same path Marietta had been taking.

"We're not going to travel with him, are we?" asked Shadowlark. "Really, Marietta, what if people start thinking we *like* him?"

"I do like him, actually," answered Marietta. "He makes me laugh. Besides, the wizard said that Frank was a good measure of how bad the Creeping Nasties have gotten. I think we should keep him with us."

Marietta ran to catch up with Frank. "So where *are* you headed?"

"That way," answered Perfectly Frank, pointing a thumb behind his back. "Only that way and nowhere else."

"Good," said Marietta, falling into step with him. "I'm headed behind me too, so we can travel together."

"You'll need me to protect you, of course," said Frank, and he moved a bit closer to Marietta. "Be sure your sword is easily reached, just in case it's needed. I mean, in case *I* need to take it to scare off a dragon or fight a duel with a villain or make sandwiches."

"In case *you* need it!" squawked the Shadowlark, rustling his feathers in indignation. "A sword in *your* hand, Frank, is a more frightening idea than being stuck with six Trolls of Questionable Origin in a small room on a hot day. In case *you* need it, indeed!" and he rustled his feathers again, just in case anyone had failed to notice him rustling them the first time.

Marietta just laughed, and they walked for awhile in silence.

They camped that night just a few hours' walk from the Illuminated Village. Marietta and Frank would take a shortcut through the

Illuminated Village, which was between them and the Bleaklands, but Shadowlark would have to fly around it. The relentless light of the Village was far more than Shadowlark could stand, and in fact they were forced to camp several miles away, where the light didn't reach.

On bright, moonlit nights, Shadowlark slept on the ground with Marietta. When the night was too dark, he had to fly to the tops of the trees where enough starlight reached him to make him comfortable. Tonight he retreated from the dark surface of the land to the very highest trees where there was enough light for him to feel safe. Marietta and Frank slept on the ground.

When Marietta woke in the morning, she called for Shadowlark to come down. She waited for several minutes, then called again, wondering if perhaps he hadn't heard her, so far up in the tips of the trees. Her calls awoke Frank, who grumbled horribly at having been wakened so early.

"Perhaps he's gone ahead," said Frank, stretching a bit and rolling up his blanket. "It's a long way around the Village."

Marietta stared at Frank in astonishment. "Frank," she said, her voice trembling a little, "what a very sensible thing to say."

Frank stopped stretching and rolling and looked back at Marietta in shock. "And completely true," said Frank, and the color drained from his face. "All of it true, every word."

"What's your name and where do you come from?" she asked him in a whisper.

"Perfectly Frank, originally from Cabbage-on-Toast," he replied immediately, his voice quivering like a dragonfly's wings. "A small farm just outside Cabbage-on-Toast, to be completely accurate."

Marietta sat on the ground with a hard *bump*, her knees having gone all shaky and wobbly. "Oh, Frank, what's happened to you?" she asked in horror.

"My lies! My lies! My beautiful lies! Someone's taken them!" Frantically he began searching on the ground around him, under his blanket, under Marietta's blanket, everywhere. "Where have they gone?"

He ran off into the woods a short way, calling for his lies just as Marietta had called for the Shadowlark a moment before.

"Shadowlark gone without saying good-bye, and now Frank telling only the truth? Something very strange is going on here," Marietta said to a small bug who was creeping through their campsite. The bug nodded in agreement and crept faster. Frank, unable to find his lies, came back to the campsite and sank slowly onto the ground like a sad, deflated balloon.

"I promise you we'll find them," she said, and she tried not to think of the many promises she had made and so far not fulfilled.

"Marietta, I've been infected with the Creeping Nasties," said Frank, his face so white Marietta could have written her homework on it. "The disease came here, right through our campsite, and took away my lies."

Marietta shivered. The disease had been that close. No wonder the fire that had burned so cheerily bright the night before now refused to light and just lay there, limp and sulking. Had she been affected? She didn't *feel* any different, but if she'd been changed, would she even know?

"We have to find the Dark Prince," said Marietta. "And Shadowlark. Will you come with me through the Illuminated Village?"

Frank nodded. Without his lies and his giggles, he seemed much older. He was a completely different person, in fact; it was as if his personality had been removed and replaced by someone else's – someone altogether ordinary and sensible. His silly lies were his joy and his life, and Marietta was suddenly struck by the thought that, without his lies, Frank himself might not live very long. This notion was rather like being stung from behind by a very large, very angry bee, and she moved even faster toward the Illuminated Village.

When they walked into the Village, the gate clanged shut behind them, and Marietta could hear Frank breathing heavily as if he had run very far or . . . as if he were very afraid.

"I shouldn't be here," he muttered, almost moaning. "Please, let's walk quickly."

Marietta nodded and stepped into the glare, her hand reaching up to shade her eyes, but of course this was impossible: there were no shadows, no shade allowed in the Illuminated Village. As soon as her hand reached her forehead, a shadow-seeking robot flew into her face and sent its bright light up under Marietta's hand to be sure that no secrets were lurking there. Marietta put her hand down, and the robot flew away. She noticed then that she seemed to be glowing, as if her body had turned to light beneath her clothes. But she quickly realized that there were hundreds of tiny shadow-seekers inside her clothes, lighting up the shadows underneath so that no pockets of darkness remained.

Marietta desperately wanted to hear the comforting voice of Shadowlark, but she knew that her friend could never exist in a place like this. Still, she could almost feel the weight of his body on her shoulder, the pressure of his claws on her skin. She hoped he was safe and knew she wouldn't be happy until she was with him again. For the first time in a long time, Marietta was afraid. Even in this land with all its light, fear cast its shadow on Marietta's heart.

"What is this place?" whispered Frank. He reached down to take Marietta's hand.

"I'm not sure," said Marietta. "All I know is that the Bleaklands lie on the other side of it somewhere, and that it will save us many days of walking to go through the Village rather than around it."

The Illuminated Village is much like any other village: there are buildings and roads and people and trees, just as there are in the place where you live. But in the Illuminated Village, everything is made of light. The buildings are crafted from shimmering light-bricks, the roads glow beneath your feet, even the trees are covered with light-leaves that fall off in autumn, when their lights begin to dim. It's a difficult place for an outsider to be because of all the light and glare, and the tourist shops are well-stocked with aspirin and cold-compresses for aching heads.

When Marietta's eyes finally got more accustomed to the light, she could begin to make out moving shapes against the buildings. She decided that these must be the residents of the Village. She approached one glow and found she was right: inside the light was a woman.

"Excuse me," Marietta said to the brightly-lit woman wrapped in illuminated robes, "We're looking for the way through the Village to the Bleaklands. Can you show us which way to go?"

"Of course," said the woman. Her voice was light and airy, just as you'd expect. "Please follow me." She led them through the winding streets of the Illuminated Village, now and again greeting another glow that passed them. Her feet didn't touch the ground as she walked; she floated an inch or two above the street, and Marietta found this a little spooky to watch. "We haven't had many visitors here of late," the woman said. "The disease of Incunabula is keeping everyone at home."

"Has it affected this place?" asked Marietta.

"Oh, yes," the woman answered, sighing. "Many people here are dimmer than they used to be. And sometimes you see a person whose light has gone a bit yellow around the edges. But I suppose we've been luckier than most places: the Illuminated Village has strong defenses. Few gain entry who don't belong." Her voice was proud.

"I see," said Marietta. "Then you really are lucky. I'm afraid my friend here was hit by the disease sometime during the night. He can no longer tell lies, you see."

The woman abruptly stopped floating, coming to a halt so fast that Marietta nearly bumped into her. "Is that Perfectly Frank you're travelling with?" she asked, pointing at Frank who was looking at his feet.

"Yes," said Marietta, and Frank nodded limply in agreement.

"Perfectly Frank in the Illuminated Village?" said the woman in shocked surprise. "But that's impossible! He shouldn't be able to come in here! I must take him directly to prism."

"Prison?" asked Marietta, holding Frank's hand tightly. "But he's done nothing wrong!"

"Not prison, *prism*," said the woman, glowing even more brightly as she spoke. "We must break him up into his component colors and see what's gone wrong." And she grabbed Frank's other hand and began pulling him quickly down a side street.

"Wait!" said Marietta, who thought this prism thing sounded horrible or at least very uncomfortable. "I don't understand! What are you doing?"

"His light! Something is wrong with his light!" said the woman, still tugging poor, listless Frank down the street.

"But we're not made of light like you are!" Marietta protested, still confused.

The woman stopped for a moment, and put one glowing hand on Marietta's shoulder. "Listen quickly, and I'll explain. Those who live in the Illuminated Village are made completely of light, but *all* creatures contain some light. And light is made up of colors: you knew that, didn't you?"

"Yeeeeeeees . . . . ," said Marietta who *had* known it once, she was sure she had.

"When someone is sick, it means one of their colors is too dim or missing altogether. So we must look at his colors and see which one is gone. The Illuminated Village is a place of perfect truth. No one ever lies here; it's forbidden. So Perfectly Frank should never have made it past the front gate. He's brought the disease into the Village, and we must do what we can to heal him before he spreads the sickness amongst us. Can you understand that?" And she started floating again, not waiting for an answer.

"But no one's been able to cure the disease," said Marietta, running to keep up. "No one at all."

"We'll do what we can. Don't worry about Frank; we'll take good care of him. Here we are."

They stopped outside a huge building; at the top was a glowing sign which read, "Village Prism." The woman opened the front door and shoved Frank inside. Frank, who was growing more and more weak and depressed from missing his wonderful lies, allowed himself to be shoved without a whimper. Marietta tried to follow, but the woman blocked her way.

"This will take some time," said the woman, holding the door so that Marietta couldn't squeeze in. "It's best if you just leave him here and let us take care of him. Come back tomorrow."

"Tomorrow! That's too late. I can't wait until tomorrow!"

"Tomorrow," the woman said, and her voice was sharp, "and not a minute before. You brought the disease to us. Allow us a chance to save ourselves." She softened, just a little. "Frank will be safe here. You must trust me." And she shut the door in Marietta's face.

Marietta sat for a moment on a glowing park bench just outside the Village Prism. Her head ached horribly from being in the Illuminated Village, and she didn't much care for the woman who had taken Frank. This may be a place of truth and light, but Marietta would have been happy to see a single shadow or hear Frank tell a silly, giggled lie. She decided to leave the Village, find Shadowlark at the meeting place, and together they would decide whether to wait for Perfectly Frank or push on into the Bleaklands without him.

On her journey through Incunabula, Marietta had met the wizard, the Moon-Shadow Tigers, the Rainbow Maker, Perfectly Frank, the boatkeeper and Nellie, the Storyteller, and of course, Shadowlark. It was strange that now, just as she was preparing to fight the biggest battle of her life, she was all alone.

Chapter Twelve

Marietta waited as long as she could at the meeting place, but finally it became clear that Shadowlark wasn't coming. She stayed there, calling his name, for several days, but she knew he was gone. Caught in a place that was too dark or too light, he had been overcome. Despite all their caution, Shadowlark had fallen victim to his own shadowy nature and disappeared.

In every life, no matter how sweetly the sword sings as it cuts the air or how softly the grass tickles bare feet, there is a time of crying, and this was Marietta's time. Each fat teardrop carried a reflection of Shadowlark's face, and she cried a thousand thousand tiny mirrors which smashed and shattered on the ground around her.

At first, the worms were driven from their tunnels for fear of drowning, but when they recognized Marietta's deep sorrow, they sang to her. They sang their blind humming song of friendship and healing; and the ants came too, and each tiny ant carried away a piece of Marietta's sadness until finally the sadness was light enough for Marietta to carry on her own. She had carried the weight of the Shadowlark on her shoulder – now she would carry the burden of his leaving in her heart.

As she was preparing to leave, the woman from the Illuminated Village appeared.

"Yellow," she said, holding out one glowing hand.

"I'm sorry?" asked Marietta, confused.

"He's missing his yellow. Frank, that is. I need your yellow bead to help him."

"Of course you do," said Marietta, unsurprised. She handed it over, wondering if *anyone else* could possibly visit the Rainbow Maker and let her keep her beads. He had pots and pots of them, after all; what was so special about hers?

Marietta continued the long journey to the Bleaklands alone, putting each foot down gently, lest too hard an impact jar loose the tears again. She was desperately lonely, thinking of Shadowlark, not knowing where he had gone. But sometimes at dawn or dusk, where night and day shake hands as they pass, she would see a shadow flicker by, just out of the range of her sight. Or when she stood for a moment in the boundarylands of light and dark, she would hear the distant echo of a familiar call. And she would feel, just for a moment, the weight of him on her shoulder and the soft pressure of his claws light against her skin, and she would hear the quiet rasp of his breathing in her ear. She would hold very still, her eyes closed, and silently promise him the Moon if only he would stay. But the Moon wasn't hers to give, and in a moment or two, the feeling would be gone.

When the Bleaklands were only a day or two away, Marietta stopped to camp for the night in the great forest that formed the wide boundary between the Bleaklands and the Illuminated Village. It was a bit colder here; not as cold as Tumble Island, but then again much colder, in a way. Where Tumble Island had snow for sledding and snowball fights and the kind of cold that makes your nose red and is best chased away by hot chocolate and a roaring fire, the cold of this place was a different kind of cold altogether.

The chill seeped into Marietta's bones, making them ache, or sat heavily on her skin, wrapping itself around her tighter than any coat or blanket. It sucked the energy out of her blood and the life from her body. Marietta didn't want to sleep for fear she wouldn't wake up in the morning, but she was exhausted from many days' travelling.

The great forest is the thickest, deepest forest in Incunabula. It was never given an official name; no name ever quite fit, and so everyone called it the 'great' forest and let it go at that. It wasn't an evil place, it just wasn't a friendly place. Marietta felt like an uninvited and not very welcome guest. The forest was polite, if such a thing may be said of a forest; nothing chased her away, but she felt as if she were constantly being watched, and she was sure all the trees and the birds and the little animals would heave a sigh of relief when she was finally gone.

She made herself a very small fire, wrapped her coat around her, and sat on the cold ground. She must have dozed off for a moment or two, for she awoke quite suddenly, her heart pounding, the echo of a sharp snap of a branch that's been stepped on still in her ear. Very very quietly, she stood and moved away from the fire, into the darkness of the forest where she couldn't be seen. From the blackness somewhere behind her came a voice:

"Why, Earthworm, you're all alone. All your friends gone? No one to talk to or play with? How very sad for our little heroine, lonely and scared in this big, dark forest with no one to protect her."

"I don't need protection, Dullard Prince," Marietta said, searching the black for the glowing eyes of the Prince. She thought perhaps one area was even darker than the darkness around it, and she moved silently towards it, her sword in one hand.

"Perfectly Frank minus a color, I wonder what's become of it? Red bead gone to save a shadowy bird, orange bead gone to find a dusty book, Frank's missing color the next bead on the string. Yellow, that's the one. I told you I would take them all, Earthworm, and take them I will."

Marietta had reached the black hole, and the stench coming from it told her the Prince was in it. She raised her sword and drove it in. There was a flash of light, and a wave like a shock of electricity travelled up Marietta's arm. There was a howl of pain and anger from inside the hole, and once again Marietta saw the *flicker*. It was as if the Prince's electricity was shut off, just for a second, and she could see the real figure of Max or *whoever* it was, crouching in the shadows behind. She was sure now that the Prince himself was nothing more than an illusion. A powerful illusion, complete with bad magic, but an illusion nonetheless.

"Not so strong after all? Not such a perfectly evil beast with no weakness, then?" Marietta took a deep breath and planted her feet firmly on the ground. She held her sword ready, if she should need it. "Hear this, Dark Prince of all that's Dull and Pointless: *I know who you are.*"

It was the scariest thing Marietta had ever done. If the Prince wasn't Max, then Marietta didn't know what he was or how to fight him. If the Dark Prince *was* Max, then telling him she knew his secret might make him murderously angry, and as the Prince, he was very powerful indeed. But Marietta stood her ground, sword raised, ready to end the chase and bring Incunabula back to health.

The Dark Prince emerged from the black hole at last: "So you think you know who I am, do you? A torn and worm-chewed book from the shelves of a crooked old man has revealed all my secrets, just like that? What's my name, Earthworm, or the color of my eyes? How tall was I when I was seven years old, and did I brush my teeth every night before I went to bed? You can know all you want about a little boy named Max, Marietta-the-would-be-hero; it won't help you at all. It's who I am *now* that makes all the difference."

His calm, quiet voice was somehow more frightening than the roar of his anger had been. It was the voice of someone with nothing to fear, and that was as bad as it could be.

"Inside the mask of the Dark Prince, you're a scared little Earth boy," said Marietta, and she was glad her voice didn't tremble.

"And how many little Earth boys have lived for five thousand years? Do you want to save the poor little boy inside, Marietta?" His voice was mocking. Marietta was stunned – how did he know everything she did, everything she thought or felt?

"That's what you've come to do, isn't it? To send Max back to the world he no longer remembers, to a life he is no longer able to live. I think not, Earthworm."

"Why do you want to destroy this place?"

The answer snapped out like a whip: "*That is no concern of yours.*"

Marietta had hit a nerve. "I can beat you," she told him. "I have friends to help me, but you fight alone."

The Dark Prince smiled. It was a smile that chilled her to the bone, so wicked and cruel was it. "Ah yes, your wonderful friends. But what has become of them all? The Shadowlark, for instance? Where *can* he have gone?" One of the Prince's hands disappeared inside his cloak. "Perhaps you recognize this?" He drew his hand out again, and in it was a single, perfect white feather – the feather from Shadowlark's breast.

The sight of that feather knocked Marietta breathless. She stood and stared at it, her eyes full of tears, unable to speak or move.

"He's not the Shadowlark anymore," said the Prince, twirling the feather in his fingers, "he's a Bleakbird now, unable to leave the dark lands where no light falls. Without this feather, he can no longer tolerate the light, so he's doomed to spend his life roaming the Bleaklands, calling the name of the little girl who should have saved him but couldn't. None of your silly little beads can give him back his light-side, you see. He's mine. And Perfectly Frank is next."

Marietta raised her sword to within an inch or two of the Dark Prince's face. He didn't pull back, didn't flinch, he just smiled that smile again.

"You think you're safe from me," Marietta whispered, for she didn't have voice enough to speak aloud. "But you have made a very grave mistake. You've forgotten what a powerful feeling love is, and how strong it can make you. If I was a weak, laughable opponent before, I fight you as your equal now."

The tingle in her arm that had first come from Incunabulan water came back again, twice as strong. She felt she could fight forever and never tire. She stood back from the Prince and held her sword level, the sharp tip of it near his heart (that is, assuming he had a heart, of course).

The Dark Prince said nothing. He just held the feather up, the bright whiteness of it casting a gentle glow on the forest around them. The Prince smiled again, and the feather burst into flames. He dropped the burning feather to the ground, and Marietta fell to her knees, beating at the flames to save Shadowlark's feather from being destroyed. Her tears nearly put out the fire before her fists did.

"One more thing, little girl," said the Prince. "I've severed every link, sealed every opening, blocked every tunnel, filled in every hole between this world and that. Except one. And do you know where that leads? Where it comes out on the other side? *Just to the left of your mirror.* What a sweet little room, what a lovely little family, what a darling little puppy. Sometimes I watch them as they sleep, Marietta; I watch your family and think how vulnerable they are. Don't get in my way. There's more to be lost here than Incunabula and a wretched little bleakbird."

Marietta leaped to her feet, but the Dark Prince was already gone. She wanted desperately to curl into a ball and cry and cry, in rage at the Prince, in terror for her family, in grief for the best friend she'd ever had, but instead she gently picked up what was left of the burnt feather and tucked it in her pocket. She fastened her sword onto her belt, returned to her campsite to put out the fire and collect the rest of her things, and headed off in the direction of the Bleaklands.

The great forest respected her sorrow, and the trees bent back to let her pass, the thorny bushes pulled their thorns aside, and the beasts of the forest left small piles of nuts and berries for her to eat. Even the fallen leaves lay so that their stems pointed in the direction she should go to reach the Bleaklands quickly. The thick, green canopy of the trees opened above her, creating holes where sunlight could shine through and warm her.

Stepping over the border into the Bleaklands is very like stepping into a vast, black hole. Where the Illuminated Village was all light, this place was all blackness, darkness so thick Marietta had to brush it away from her face like cobwebs. There was a path that led directly to the palace of the Dark Prince of Dullardry. He wasn't hiding, that was for sure: signs littered the path, signs with letters that glowed like the Prince's eyes. "*This way to the End of Incunabula, Marietta,*" one sign read, and another, a few feet on: "*Turn back to save your pitiful life; only failure lies ahead.*" Marietta stubbornly ignored the signs and continued on the path, despite glowing warnings such as, "*The further you go, the bigger fool you are.*"

The blackness of the Bleaklands swallowed her up. When she looked back the way she had come, she couldn't see the great forest or the light of the world outside this envelope of darkness. She held her sword tightly in one hand, and with the other, she frequently checked to be sure the string of remaining beads were firmly around her neck. The beads glowed slightly, as if they had caught a bit of the light of the Illuminated Village. Marietta was glad, for they lit her way. She suspected they had always glowed, but she hadn't noticed before because there was always greater light around.

Marietta realized that the coldness she'd felt in the great forest had leaked over there from here. This place was bone-numbingly, brain-chillingly *cold*. The ice that had lodged in Max's heart had spread over his domain.

Perhaps, thought Marietta, *he has to be kept at a freezing temperature or else he would rot.* Marietta rather suspected he already had.

She was just chopping a sign into bits with her sword ("*What's a single feather, between friends?*"), when she felt the pressure of a familiar weight perch lightly on her shoulder. She stood absolutely still and held her breath.

"I don't suppose you have any purple berries on you?" rasped a much-loved voice in her ear.

"I do, actually." She had collected many of Shadowlark's favorite berries in the great forest, and the little animals had left more on the trail for her. She pulled these out of her pocket and handed them to the bird on her shoulder. "Can you . . . can you stay with me?"

"As long as you're here in the Bleaklands, I can," the Shadowlark replied. "Once you step outside its boundaries, I can no longer follow."

Shadowlark flew to a nearby sign ("*You really know how to pick your heroines, Bleakbird!*") and perched on it. He looked small and vulnerable without his white feather. The place on his breast where the feather had been looked empty, wounded. But his eyes were the same and the dark sparkles in them were the same, and Marietta hugged him tightly.

"Oh, Shadowlark, it's all my fault!" she cried. "I was supposed to save you, that was our agreement. I'm so sorry-"

"Really, Marietta, how could a clumsy, Earthbound creature like you save me from a villain who lurks at the top of the tallest trees? As Billy-down-the-block knows, climbing trees was never your strong suit." And his sweet, brittle, forgiving laugh brought tears to her eyes. He flew back to perch on her shoulder.

"The fight isn't over yet," she said. She paused until she could be sure her tears wouldn't be heard in her voice. "I've missed you."

"Yes, I suspected you would," replied the bird, and he bit down on the first of the berries with a loud crunch. "I've missed you too."

Not long after this, they came to a river. Well, it *looked* like a river, but it was really an inlet of the other half of Divided Ocean, the part that disappeared at Half-Land. River or inlet, half an ocean or all of it, it was a long way across, and Marietta had no boat.

"Now what?" Marietta sat on a rock just at the edge of the water. She put her elbows on her knees and her chin on her palms and felt utterly depressed and defeated. "There's no way across."

"No way at all," said a voice from somewhere nearby.

Marietta started, jolted by the unexpected voice. "Hello?" She strained her eyes in the darkness.

"Don't bother looking, I can't be seen, not even by your bleakbird," said the voice. "I'm invisible now, blast it, and have been since the

Land of Infinite Variations. A place to avoid, if you're at all content with who you are."

"I'm sorry. Will nothing make you visible again?" From the sound of the voice, the speaker had sat down on the rock next to Marietta.

"I've no idea."

"Why do you stay here, in the Bleaklands? There are happier places to be."

"With the Creeping Nasties lurking all around? No, at least this place is safe from the disease. It's been diseased from the beginning, so nothing changes here. Besides, any change in *this* place would be for the better."

"My name is Marietta."

"Mistress of Tides," came the response. "You're the hero from Earth. I'm supposed to try and stop you, you know. I have orders to pull back the waters and let you get partway across before flooding you and sweeping you to your death."

"I . . . I'd rather you didn't," said Marietta, unsure how to respond politely to such a remark.

"I've really no choice. So sorry. But you can stay here, with me. I'm not such interesting company, but surely I'm better than dying?"

"Actually," said Marietta, hesitantly, "I was going to come looking for you, eventually."

"Well, you wouldn't have found me, not in my present condition."

"No, that's true." Marietta paused, not knowing if this was a good time to say what she wanted to say. "I want to petition you on behalf of a friend."

"Oh? Go on."

"Her name is Nellie. She was a horse. Now she's a boat. I'd like her to be a horse again, if you wouldn't mind reversing your spell."

"Oh, yes. I remember her. Stupid nag nearly trampled me. What's in it for me if I turn her back?"

Marietta sighed. "I don't know. It seems I've made so many promises to help people, and I've done so little. I suppose I could give you one of my beads. I've got four left."

"A rainbow bead? Ooooo, yes!. I could take it to the Prince, and he would reward me."

An idea popped suddenly in Marietta's head, the lightbulb of it illuminating the dark corners of her unhappiness. "Yes. A green bead for nature, for returning a living creature to the way she was. Please."

"Give it to me!" the witch demanded, and so, with trembling fingers, Marietta again untied the string and released one of her rainbow beads. As soon as she handed it to the Mistress of Tides, the bead became invisible. A moment later, a young woman appeared. Marietta was startled at how *normal* the Mistress of Tides looked. She had long blond hair tucked behind her ears, glasses halfway down a long, sharp nose, and she wore a simple black dress that reached past her feet to drag on the ground. One clenched fist glowed slightly green between the fingers.

Without another word, the witch turned and waved an arm at the water, which separated at her command. As the witch hurried across, eager to present the bead to the Prince, she didn't even notice Marietta trailing close behind. As they reached the other side, Marietta ducked quickly behind a rotted tree stump. The witch turned and waved again at the water, and the gap closed with a thunderous crash and waves giant enough to sweep away a village. It had cost her a bead, but Marietta was across, and with any luck, Nellie was again the shape she'd been born in. Three beads left.

Marietta tried to follow the witch through the Bleaklands to the palace of the Prince, but in her black dress, the Mistress of Tides quickly disappeared in the darkness. However, Marietta was no longer alone. Shadowlark crunched quietly in her ear. Neither of them spoke, but both of them had the same thought: once Incunabula was saved, *if* it was saved, then Marietta would leave the Bleaklands, and she and Shadowlark would be separated forever. It was a thought as cold and dark as the land around them, and it weighed too heavily on their hearts to be spoken. Marietta was even a bit glad for all the darkness: it hid her tears.

Chapter Thirteen

Blue, indigo and violet. The last three beads on the chain were all at the darker end of the color spectrum, the colors that formed the underbelly of the rainbow, heavier with color than the lighter red, orange, yellow and green. Marietta's fingers kept coming back to the beads around her neck, toying with them, rolling them between her fingertips, tugging lightly at the string to test its strength.

"What I don't understand," said the Shadowlark, between purple-berry crunches, "is why the Rainbow Maker didn't just give you a whole *pot* of the silly things. He has enough, that much is certain; so why only one of each? And if the beads are so powerful, why doesn't he fight the Dark Prince himself? Really, Marietta, you must learn to ask the appropriate questions."

"I trusted the Rainbow Maker to know what he was doing, Shadowlark," answered Marietta. "I still do. I don't think he was giving me *beads*, really; I think he was giving me some of his magic. The beads were just a convenient way for me to carry them, you see? And probably he only had a little bit of magic to give."

"So the beads are nothing more than envelopes or shopping bags?"

"Exactly. They are very beautiful, very wonderful envelopes and shopping bags. Or something like that. But it makes sense, doesn't it?"

"Mmmmm. What do you suppose magic looks like, then? Does it come in a tablet? Or powder form? Perhaps in a liquid that you pour onto a spoon to swallow? Is it bitter? Sour? Sweet? Does it make you lick your lips or wrinkle your nose?"

"I don't think magic is like medicine."

"But both can cure us when we're ill."

"Perhaps you're right, Shadowlark. I wish we could look it up in the wizard's notebook; I'm sure he's written about it. But it's too dark here to read."

"Not for me, it isn't. Not any more."

There was a long pause. Walking and talking together, even in this horrible place, was so natural to Marietta that, for a time, she had forgotten that Shadowlark was changed. She fought to swallow the lump in her throat that threatened to choke her.

"Will you read to me what the wizard has written?"

"Certainly." And the Shadowlark fetched the wizard's notebook from Marietta's pocket and began rummaging through the pages. "A table of contents, I think, would not be too much to ask," he grumbled, flipping backwards and forwards through the notebook. "Ahhh. Here we are."

Some Preliminary Notes on the Nature of Magic:

Magic is a bit like water, or perhaps even more like air, in that it can take any form, change its shape to fit its circumstances, expand to fit inside big places, or shrink to cram itself into tiny places. It has no shape of its own, in fact: no color, no smell, no taste, it makes no sound. It is not poisonous if swallowed, but it can be dangerous in many other ways. Magic exists to serve — that is its purpose. Just as air exists to be breathed and water to be drunk or bathed in or washed with, just as sunlight exists to make things grow, magic is a necessary part of the structure of things. But, as air fills the lungs of the good and the evil alike, and as sunlight nourishes the bodies and spirits of the kind and the cruel, so magic will serve both fair purposes and foul, without judgement, without hesitation.

Perhaps the most important thing to know about magic is that it gives as it takes. This is where it differs from water and from air. Both water and air are finite: that is to say, when they are used up, they are gone. Magic, on the other hand, can grow. If it is used correctly, magic increases; it becomes bigger and stronger. Those who use magic selfishly and do not respect its power, use it up. Those who understand that a little bit of magic can go a long way will discover that magic spent returns, with interest.

Marietta walked along the path, deep in silence and thought. Shadowlark, having returned the wizard's notebook to Marietta's pocket, resumed his place on Marietta's shoulder and his regular rhythm of crunching in her ear.

"Was all that important, do you think?" he asked finally, tired of the silence. His mouth was really a bit full for polite conversation, and he dribbled a seed or two on Marietta's shirt. He was quietly glad that it was too dark for Marietta to see the stain.

"Yes," Marietta said at last. "I think perhaps it was." And that was all she said, for a very long while.

The closer they got to the Dark Prince's palace, the colder the world around them became. At night they huddled together under Marietta's coat. Shadowlark wasn't actually cold, since he now belonged here in the Bleaklands, but he didn't mention that to Marietta because he knew it would make her sadder.

Being a resident of the Bleaklands had given Shadowlark a different kind of sight, a sight that was sensitive to all kinds of light, not just light from lamps or the sun. He could see the light that Marietta gave off – a sweet white glow with bits of pink and blue around the edges. And every time she remembered that Shadowlark was banished to the Bleaklands forever, that light dimmed a bit, lost some of its radiance and cheer, and that made Shadowlark afraid. She would need all her light to protect her here, so even though the coat threatened to suffocate him with its heat and weight every night, he gladly submitted to being covered if it helped keep Marietta's light safe.

One night it was so cold that even Marietta's coat wasn't enough to keep her warm. She tried to make a fire, but of course, that was impossible. She sat and shivered, all night, in front of a pile of sticks that wouldn't burn. She was so exhausted, so worn, that a heavy tread behind her in the darkness hardly frightened her at all.

It was one of the tigers. Marietta was shocked at seeing one alone, clear out here in the Bleaklands. She was even more shocked when the tiger came closer, and Marietta could see how ragged and filthy her fur was and how thin she looked.

"What's happened to you?" she whispered, horrified.

"We found a tunnel, from Incunabula to Earth," answered the tiger, her voice sounding so starved, Marietta could see its ribs. "Or at least, we thought we did. Once inside, we found the Earth side had been sealed. When we tried to return, the Incunabulan end was also blocked. We dug for many days to make a hole big enough for me to squeeze through, but my mate is still trapped. I came to find you, Marietta. And to beg you for a bead."

"No, please no, don't beg!" cried Marietta. "Take the bead, hurry! Free him before he starves! Incunabula can't survive without both of its tigers." Marietta tore off the necklace, nearly breaking the thread in her haste. She pulled off the blue bead and handed it to the tiger who nodded her thanks and fled, back the way she had come. Marietta, shaken to her core, fell to her knees.

"One by one, he takes my beads from me," Marietta whispered to herself and the sleeping form of the Shadowlark. "If I have none left, how will I save Incunabula? Oh, Shadowlark, if I have none left, how will I save *you?*" And she lay awake until the thicker darkness was replaced by the thinner darkness, the exchange of colors that passed for dawn in that lightless place.

The indigo bead fell to the Dark Prince the following day. A vision of the tumble-down wizard, his long robe tangling around his feet and tripping him up as the Creeping Nasties approached to engulf him, forced Marietta to crunch the second-to-last bead to dust underneath her foot. The magic of the indigo bead made the wizard sure-footed, and for the first time since he'd left Tumble Island, he was able to run like the wind without falling headfirst down a hole or stumbling over a leaf that wasn't lying perfectly flat.

This time, Marietta didn't hesitate at all. She knew the bead would be sacrificed somehow, to help someone sooner or later, and she gave it up almost without a thought. It was simply a question of time before the last bead on the string was taken.

It seemed almost that the Dark Prince had spoken the truth: friends did make one weak and vulnerable. It had been terribly easy for him to take her beads from her, after all. He simply threatened those she loved, and she gave up the required beads to save them. But she knew that couldn't be right. There had to be more to it than that, if only she could figure out the secret. She spent much of the journey to the palace thinking on this question and wiping berry seeds from her shirtfront.

Finally, Marietta and Shadowlark reached the steps that led into the Dark Prince's palace itself. The palace was exactly what Marietta had expected: it was dark and scary, it loomed and lurched over her, and black flashes of lightening whipped and snapped around its tall towers. It was a hunched, squatted toad of a castle in front, with great tall turrets behind that seemed to rip the dark sky open with their sharp tips.

It did all those things that the palace of the villain is supposed to do, in short: it moaned and whistled, it housed nasty winged creatures that flapped and flolloped their way around and between the towers, it *leaned* as if it would reach down a thick, stone arm to crush Marietta where she stood. And everywhere was the sound of sadness. Marietta had never known that sadness made a noise, but it did. It was a thick, heavy sort of noise that covered her like a blanket, wrapped around her like a shroud. It was as wet as tears, as thick as grief, as hazy as lost hopes and shattered dreams. Marietta could hardly walk under the weight of that sadness, with the sound of it heavy in her ears. She struggled up the front steps of the castle, determined to find the Prince and end this.

It wasn't hard. The Dark Prince stood at the foot of the grand staircase that led into the upper reaches of the castle. He smiled a huge, welcoming smile; a smile that obviously expected an easy victory. He came down to Marietta, and putting his thin, bony finger to her throat, he lifted the string to see the last lonely bead that still hung on it.

"Ahhhhh, violent violet, such a lovely color; the last letter of the Rainbow Maker's name. Will you give it to me now, Earthworm, or shall I torture one of your friends for it first? Let's see, who remains? Nellie has her shape back, and Perfectly Frank has returned to telling lies that fool no one. The scribbling wizard is safe for the moment from my marvelous Nasties, and the Shadowlark, well, perhaps the violet bead will keep him in purple berries for the rest of his miserable, Bleak life."

Marietta untied the string from her neck and pulled the final bead loose. It sat on her palm, giving off a faint violet glow and a tiny violet hum.

"Go," she said to the bead in a quiet voice. "Go before the Prince takes you, too."

And as the Dark Prince watched in shocked silence, the bead rose from Marietta's palm and floated in the air for a second or two before shooting away so fast that it left a light-trail of violet behind it, like a shooting star.

"That was very foolish of you," said the Prince, and his eyes glowed angrily. "But it doesn't matter. Now you have no protection. The battle is over. I had hoped for a bit more competition from you, but it doesn't matter. It's too late for the Incunabulans to bring another child from Earth, so Incunabula is *mine*." The Prince turned and began to walk up the long staircase, but at about the fourth step, he found he couldn't continue. When he turned around to look, he discovered Marietta had pinned his cape to the ground with the tip of her sword.

"I told you once I needed no protection, Prince. The beads weren't intended to provide me with magic, they were meant to teach me a lesson. And they did."

"And what lesson is that?" hissed the Prince, tugging at his cape and finally tearing it free with a loud *riiiiip!* "What is it that you think you understand?"

"Magic is both the disease and the cure, that's what I learned. That if you use it correctly, with love and respect, magic heals, magic builds. If you use it carelessly, even if you don't mean to, magic corrupts and magic destroys. I learned that from the Trolls of Tumble Island. I didn't know that my imagination turned to magic over here, and so when I was careless, I created something nasty and horrible. But when I knew how to use my magic, I could build beautiful castles in the sky and help my friends when they needed me."

"How lovely," said the Prince sarcastically. "So if I would just turn my magic to goodness and light, all would be well, is that it? Perhaps I could make magic that would braid ribbons in little girls' hair, or make limp, greasy bunnies all fluffy and soft again. Even more exciting, I could charm the worms right out of the apples. I could mend this tear you've made in my cape, and make the sweetest-tasting chocolate widgets this side of the Divided Ocean. How delightful."

"Sure," said Marietta, "you could do all those things, if that's as far as your imagination reaches. Personally, I find there are lots more exciting things out there to do." She held her sword up above her head. "Like fighting evil Princes and saving worlds from destruction." Her eyes sparkled and there was a little smile on her face. She shook off the cloak of sadness. "It's time to finish the battle, Prince of All Things Pointless. Shall we?"

There was a *flicker*, even shorter than previous *flickers*, but it was there. Marietta felt the strength of Incunabula pouring down her arm and flooding her body. Even if her sword had suddenly turned back into a fish, she felt, she would still win this fight. In the next instant, the Dark Prince of Dullardry raised his sword, a sharp, evil-looking thing that glinted blackly in the darkness of the room. Their swords clashed, Marietta's making a sharp, clear ringing sound like a bell; the Prince's chiming like a death knell. Shadowlark flew from Marietta's shoulder to perch on the unused chandelier high above, trying not to tangle himself in the thick cobwebs that stretched around it.

Up and down the staircase, the battle raged. Marietta fought as if she had been born to hold a sword. She whirled and twirled and leapt like a tornado on the ground. The Dark Prince was a vicious opponent. If he couldn't knock the sword from Marietta's hand, he tried to knock her feet out from under her. He called upon the nasty, winged creatures that lived in the high towers to help him, but Shadowlark battled with these, sending more than a few back to their nests with singed and broken feathers.

At one point, Marietta turned and raced to the top of the stairs, then slid back to the Prince down the bannister, her sword in front of her like a lance. The Prince stood frozen to the spot, watching her advance like a Moon-Shadow Tiger sliding down a moonbeam. He leapt out of the way at the very last second, Marietta's sword tearing a fresh hole in his coat.

"When you are my prisoner, Earthworm, your first task will be to mend the holes you've made in my clothes." He stood, panting, black rivulets of sweat running down his face. Then he brought up his sword in one vicious swipe, and the battle began again.

The fight lasted many hours, as is recorded in the Incunabulan history books. For a time, it was clear that Marietta would defeat the Prince. Then the tide of the battle turned, and the Prince's victory seemed inevitable. But Marietta found new strength in the voice of the Shadowlark who called to her from above, and the fight turned again. The great staircase of the palace was nearly destroyed in the fighting: the railing and steps were shattered by blows from the swords.

The nasty winged creatures took fright both from the sounds of the fury below, and also from the pecking they'd received from the Shadowlark; they flew away to an even deeper part of the Bleaklands, never to return.

So evenly matched were the opponents, the fight might still be continuing today, if Marietta hadn't shouted out: "All this, because you were *ashamed?*"

Immediately, the Dark Prince *flickered* and crumpled a little around the edges, but still he kept fighting.

"What do you mean 'ashamed,' you ridiculous slug?" he shouted. "Save your breath for the battle."

"Ashamed of your imagination!" Marietta called out, her voice barely audible above the clash of their swords. "Ashamed to find it so pitiful and weak!"

There was another *flicker*, and this time Marietta clearly saw the little boy behind, just for a moment.

"I don't know what you mean," said the Prince. "Now, shut up and fight."

Suddenly Marietta threw her sword across the room. It stuck in the wall, quivering like an arrow that's been shot from a powerful bow. "No," she said. And she stood very still.

The Prince, for lack of an opponent, stopped fighting too. For a moment, the room was filled with the sound of their gasping as they tried to get their breath back.

"Answer me this:" said Marietta, when she had voice enough to speak, "if there is chocolate in a chocolate bar, if a crystal ball really is made of crystal, then how much water does it take to make a water buffalo?"

"What? What are you talking about?"

"Answer me, Max, if you can; there's snow in a snowman, but how many angels in an angelfood cake? How much fire in a firefly, and why doesn't it burn him from inside? *You don't know, do you?!* But *I* know the answer. I have imagination enough for any question you ask. Perhaps the answer isn't right; maybe the question is foolish and no answer exists. But that doesn't matter – what matters is not the answer but the *answering,* the imagination, the dream, the fantasy. Normal and ordinary and sensible are important, but magic also has its place. And that's what you hate most about me, about this place, isn't it? It's the magic that you lack. You're a Dullard, Max, and you know it, and *that* has made you cruel."

"I'll carve you to pieces!" roared the Prince, and his eyes shot sparks, and the very blackness of him seemed to swell and grow in his fury.

"Marietta, what are you doing!" squawked Shadowlark from above. "He'll kill you!"

"I don't think so, Shadowlark," Marietta answered. "It's all right; just be still."

"You don't know me!" cried the Prince, raising his sword high. "You don't know what cruelties I am capable of!"

"Oh, Max, come on," said Marietta, smiling a little. "I know you. You're such a *good* boy."

Insane with rage, the Prince screamed at the heavens and charged directly at Marietta, his sword sizzling hot in his angry hand.

Marietta had gambled and lost, and so she stayed still, her eyes shut, expecting at any moment for the sword to pierce her heart. But it never came. For Shadowlark, desperate to save the girl he had so grown to love, had flown directly at the Prince, intent on stopping him. But before he could, the Dark Prince caught him with the flat of his sword, knocking him across the room where he smacked into a wall and fell into a crumpled heap on the floor, lifeless.

"*No!*" Marietta screamed, running over to lift the shattered body in her arms. "Oh, Shadowlark, why did you do that?" She rocked back and forth on her knees, weeping and stroking Shadowlark's feathers. He was dead.

"I told you not to challenge me," said the Prince, his sword high in the air, ready to strike Marietta down. "Incunabula will be mine, or it will be nothing at all."

Tears pouring down her face, Marietta clutched the limp, breathless body of the Shadowlark to her chest. "*You,*" she said to the Prince, "you are nothing at all. The Incunabulans, they think that Incunabula has all the magic and Earth has none, but they're wrong. Imagination *is* Earth magic. You have no imagination, no magic at all, not here and not at home, so you steal it from others. But stolen magic is bad, and it corrupts the one who stole it." Marietta stood up, still cradling Shadowlark in her arms. The Prince seemed frozen, his sword still in midair. "Magic must be freely given, in the service of others. Like the beads which were given to me and which I gave away to save my friends. You use stolen magic for your own desires. And look what it has gotten you: power, but no friends. A castle, but no kingdom. You've caused death and destruction and sadness so great it has a *sound*. Are you proud of what you've become?" She held out the lifeless body of Shadowlark. "Are you proud of what you've done?"

Marietta, her strength totally gone, sank down on the bottom stair. She held Shadowlark to her face and wept. *Let the Prince strike,* she thought. *There's no damage he can do greater than this.*

But the Prince didn't strike. He crumpled. As if his legs had disappeared beneath him, he tumbled, his cape covering him. He shrank down to a small, golden-haired little boy in a cape that dragged on the floor behind him and boots that nearly came to his hips. His face was pale and sad, his voice a whisper.

"I'm sorry. I'm so sorry. I'd save him if I could."

Suddenly, beneath her tears, Marietta remembered the white rose that the Queen of Quiet Mountain had given her. She reached deep into her pocket where it lay, forgotten for all this time. It was dry and dead, but it was still very beautiful and smelled as sweet as the day she'd picked it. She lay the flower on Shadowlark's breast, and held him tightly to her. It was all she could do. She knelt on the ground for a long time, holding the tiny body of the bird, not even noticing when Shadowlark first rustled his wings in impatience.

"You can let me go now," he croaked in his rusty voice. "It's quite difficult to breathe down here."

"Shadowlark?" she whispered, not believing it could be true. But when she opened her arms, he flew an awkward lap around the room and came to rest in his usual place on her shoulder. The flower from the Queen had disappeared – it had turned into a white feather, replacing the feather that the Dark Prince had stolen and burned. Shadowlark was alive and a Bleakbird no more.

"It's very dark in here," said the bird. "Perhaps we should go."

The Dark Prince was gone, and Max was once again a little boy from Earth. He led Marietta quickly from the palace. In a conventional fairy tale land, it would transpire that when the Dark Prince disappeared, so the Bleaklands changed into a place of light and color, but that didn't happen here. It *did* change, actually, but in an odd way. The dark changed from a threatening, evil sort of dark, to a comforting, fun sort of dark like you find under your blankets during a slumber party or in your parents' tent when camping in the woods. There's nothing wrong with blackness or darkness, after all; only with the things that lurk in it, and use it as cover. Those things disappeared, or retreated further into the Bleaklands, and the area around the palace became the best place in Incunabula for a really good game of hide-and-go-seek.

Marietta was anxious about getting Shadowlark out of the Bleaklands before the darkness caught up with him, but she needn't have worried. The violet bead she'd set free had gone directly to the Rainbow Maker's workshop, and was now returning, dragging a huge, thickly-colored rainbow behind it. The light it cast made shadows enough for the Shadowlark to be comfortable, and its colors spread to where no colors had been for many long centuries.

Marietta and Max sat on the grass underneath the rainbow, Marietta enjoying the first light and color she'd seen in quite a while. Max blinked a lot and stared at his shoes.

"How did you know?" Max asked finally. "How did you figure out I had no magic of my own?"

"It just finally made sense," Marietta answered. She lay on her back in the grass, trying to count the beads in the rainbow above – a wonderfully pointless and impossible task. "Who else would choose to be the Dark Prince of Dullardry but a Dullard? I figured it out when I saw the trolls and the umbrella bats. They were *mine*, and they made me feel connected. I had to protect this place because a part of me lived here. I figured that when you got here, there were no creatures from your imagination to meet up with: no castle in the sky, not even a flower in the Queen's garden, nothing. It was as foreign as Mars to you. And you were ashamed that you had no imagination, that you didn't really belong here. Am I close?"

Max nodded but didn't speak for a long moment. "I was a Dullard," he said at last. "And I knew it. I didn't want to be, but I was stuck, and I couldn't get out of it. Then everybody here thought I was such a great hero, saving the land from the winter creatures, but all the time I knew I shouldn't be here, like Perfectly Frank in the Illuminated Village. I felt so stupid, and then I got mad. I knew what I was doing was wrong, but it felt *good* to be the Dark Prince. Building this palace, figuring out ways to change everything, stuff like that. I kind of lost control of the Dark Prince, though. I didn't mean to be *so* bad, just a little bad, maybe." He shrugged. "Now I'll have to go back to being dull little Max-he's-such-a-*good*-boy. Ugh."

"Max, haven't you been paying attention at all?" Marietta sat up and looked him in the eye. "Anybody who can dream up the Dark Prince isn't dull at all." She threw a handful of grass at him. "Are boys born stupid, or do they get stupider as they get older?"

On their way out of the Bleaklands, they met up with the wizard and the Moon-Shadow Tigers. The tigers, still weak and much too thin, were going to take Max back to Earth. Now that the ice had melted, he was free to go home.

"I haven't seen my folks in five thousand years. Weird, huh?" He turned to the tigers. "I've done a lot of apologizing lately, and I have about a thousand years' worth left to do. For what it's worth, I'm sorry."

Perhaps a bit too roughly, the she-seeming tiger flipped the boy up on her back. "Hold on," she growled. "This may be a bumpy ride." She winked at Marietta, and the tigers were gone, bearing Max away.

"He's not really a good little boy at all, is he?" Marietta asked the wizard, a smile on her face.

"So many are fooled by bright eyes and shiny smiles," said the wizard. "I imagine he'll make his share of trouble in life."

"By the way," said Marietta, and she blushed a little, "I know where the Trolls of Questionable Origin came from."

"Oh? Mmmmmm," he said, not really paying attention, for a sky-castle had just floated into view. "Incunabula is recovering," he said, pointing. "Every minute, some wonderful new thing appears, or some wonderful old thing reappears. We owe you a great deal, Marietta. A great deal, indeed."

Marietta reached up to hand Shadowlark another bunch of purple berries. Her heart still thumped every time she thought of how she had nearly lost him.

"Never mind, wizard," she said, brushing seeds from her hair. "I have everything I need."

Chapter Fourteen

The celebration held in Marietta's honor and to celebrate the end of the Dark Prince and his Creeping Nasties lasted for many days. First there was a procession, held at the palace of the Queen of Quiet Mountain. She had decided, flower or no flower, to come out of her castle at last and be part of the festivities. Her steps were unsteady as she left the palace where she had been the willing captive of her heart for over four hundred years, but her voice was strong, and her eyes were joyful. She stood at the front of her palace and waited for Marietta to come.

Never had the garden of Quiet Mountain looked so beautiful, and the garden was a place known for its eye-blurring beauty. The servants of the Queen had spent the last week frantically throwing kisses to replace the flowers lost to the Creeping Nasties. They had thrown kisses to everyone: family, friends, perfect strangers on the street. Rumor had it that a Giant Fuzzball had been attacked with so many thrown kisses from a band of kitchen-helpers that it melted right down into a bunny rabbit with a bad case of static cling, in front of their startled eyes. Certainly, with so many kisses bouncing through the air like rubber balls, many new romances had blossomed alongside the flowers. The garden was so full of flowers there wasn't much room for people to stand and watch the procession, so the Queen had ordered her floating spectator stands brought out, and the whole ceremony would take place in the air, just above the tops of the tallest flowers.

Marietta arrived in a bubble-carriage pulled by Nellie and her mounted lamp-keeper who had been borrowed from the Queen of Half-Land for this very special day.

"The uniform still fits, see if it doesn't!" the former boatkeeper had shouted at her as they hitched her bubble to the horse.

The boatkeeper, when he still *was* a boatkeeper, hadn't told Marietta that Nellie was no ordinary horse. She was a fleethorse: a winged horse of exceptional power and beauty. She was charcoal, midnight, dark-chocolate *black*, so beautifully black that she out-glowed the lamps and the flowers and the Queen herself. Great, powerful black wings, each longer than Marietta was tall, grew from either side of her broad back, and her mane was black silk fringed with fire. Nellie was magnificent, and she took Marietta's breath away. Shyly, feeling incredibly stupid, Marietta pulled an apple from her pocket and handed it to the horse.

"I wanted to keep my promise," she said, by way of excuse.

Nellie took the apple in her mouth, and with a *crunch* equal to ten thousand purple-berry crunches, she bit it in two and ate it. When the apple was gone, Nellie gently nuzzled Marietta with a nose as soft as only horse-noses can be.

"When the witch turned me into a boat," said Nellie, and her voice was music, her words running up and down the scale like a virtuoso on a violin, "she took more from me than my legs and my mane. She took my wings, Marietta, she stole my sky. I am sometimes a creature of the ground, just as you can swim happily in water for a time. But the ground is not where I live. I am a creature of the air; that is my element and my home. And water, well . . . " and here the mighty horse shivered, setting dark rays of light dancing as they flickered, reflected by the gloss of her mane, "water is like poison to me. If a boat could die, I surely would have. You have given me back the air, Marietta, and wings to fly it with. It is with great pride and gratitude that I pull your carriage today." And here the fleethorse lay her giant head atop Marietta's much smaller one – the horse equivalent of a hug.

That thing, whatever that thing is, that rises in the throat when you are overcome with emotion, well, it was back in Marietta's throat now, and no amount of swallowing could get rid of it. So she only nodded and stroked Nellie's elegant black mane for a moment before climbing into the bubble-carriage with the wizard and Shadowlark.

Fitting for a procession that would take place in the sky, the bubble-carriage was exactly what it sounds like: a carriage in a bubble, made especially to be drawn through the air by a fleethorse.

Marietta felt incredibly silly sitting in this thing that should either be coming from a schoolgirl's mouth, since it looked exactly like a bubble-gum bubble, or sitting atop a wedding cake, perhaps. The bubble itself was a faint pink, the color so faint that people could easily see through it to the people inside.

The carriage, well . . . the carriage was Marietta's ultimate nightmare: it was white with bits of gold stuck all over the place and *fussy*. The inside seats were the pink of a little girl's doll, it was all gooey and regal and overdone and yeeeeeuuuuch. It was fairy-tale in the extreme, but not the kind of fairy-tales Marietta liked. This carriage would be at home in a story that ended in a wedding and a kiss, and Marietta could think of nothing worse, or at least nothing stickier.

It was something Cinderella sat in on her wedding day, Marietta thought (and indeed, she was right, but she didn't know that); *I'd much rather be riding between Nellie's wings.*

But she sat calmly and smiled and waved at the crowds that filled the floating stands and threatened to sink them. The sky overhead was filled with castles, and Marietta spotted the one she herself had made. Everyone was there that day: the Rainbow Maker had filled every inch of available sky with rainbows, the Storyteller had a group of children gathered around him and was telling them a story that made them shiver and laugh, and, judging from the occasional chestnut that popped out from the trees overhead, even the Chestnut Trolls had left the flatlands and climbed the mountain to see the parade. The Moon-Shadow Tigers, returned from their journey to Earth, sat on either side of the palace steps, their tails curled around them, their fur shining. Marietta thought that nothing in the world could be so beautiful, so breath-stoppingly beautiful as a Moon-Shadow Tiger or a fleethorse.

Nellie carried Marietta proudly to the palace gate, the lamp-keeper sitting tall on her back and holding his lamp high. They were off soon to fight in the battle of the Great Jeweled Falls of Fought-About River, but that is another story entirely.

When the carriage reached the palace, the Under Carriage Deputy pulled the bubble over to the palace steps where the Queen waited, and let the air out of the bubble so that the carriage could rest on the ground.

The air, coming from the bubble, made a rather ridiculous sound, and Marietta and the wizard and Shadowlark sat in the carriage and laughed until their stomachs hurt as the noise went on and on, and the rest of Incunabula waited in embarrassed silence for it to end. Finally the bubble was deflated, unzipped, and lifted away from the carriage. Marietta, with Shadowlark on her shoulder, jumped quickly to the ground. The wizard, of course, didn't so much jump as *plummet*, but fortunately, the deflated bubble around the carriage made a nice cushion, and he wasn't hurt at all.

The Queen of Quiet Mountain came forward to present Marietta with a medal. It was the highest medal that Incunabula awarded, and its name was *Chimera*.

"With this medal," said the Queen, her voice so soft that the entire world leaned forward to hear her better, "all of Incunabula is open to you. You may go where you wish, live as you like, do what you please. As long as you act with a kind and honest heart, you are welcome in every corner of this land. And when you are home on Earth, this medal makes it possible for you to come here again, as often as you like, for as long as you wish. It is called the Chimera, because that mythical beast was made of many parts: the head of a lion, the body of a goat, the tail of the serpent. So do imagination and magic have many parts, some noble, some not. Chimera will never let you forget the lessons you learned here. But Chimera can also mean a fancy, a dream, an imagining." And here the Queen smiled, perhaps her first real smile in four hundred years, and it was spectacular. "And these are central to Incunabula, to its strength and its magic."

The Queen bid Marietta come forward, and she put the medal around Marietta's neck. At that moment, as arranged, the rainbows of the Rainbow Maker let down their beads in a multicolored shower from the sky. The beads fell like confetti, popping just before they hit the ground. It was a fantastic sight, the sky filled with rainbow beads, and the people of Incunabula let out a whoop of joy that set the castles in the sky bouncing and bumping into one another. But no one minded. When there was quiet again, the Queen addressed the Shadowlark.

"You made the greatest of sacrifices to save your friend," said the Queen, "and magic saved your life. You are now a creature of magic, and thus you will become the greatest Sorcerer and teacher of magic this land has ever known. With your shadowy nature, one wing equally in light and dark, you are the best to teach us about the dual nature of magic. Will you teach us?"

"I will," said the Shadowlark, in his rusty, rattly voice. Marietta had never seen him stand so straight and tall. The Queen put another medal around Shadowlark's neck, and there was a second whoop and roar from the crowd. When all was silent again, the Queen bid the wizard come forward. After he had been pulled off the ground, and the six ministers of agriculture, education, magic, fire, water, and light had been helped up, and the chairs righted and the candles relit, and the Queen herself had dusted the wizard's footprint off her dress, and the general havoc caused by the wizard's fall was fixed, he stood in front of the Queen, trembling.

"Stumbling, tumble-down wizard, I wish I could give you balance," said the Queen with a smile, and the audience roared with laughter, "but that is beyond my power. Instead I give you two gifts: one, the forgiveness of the people of Tumble Island. You are free to return home any time you like, and none will trouble you over the misfortunes of the past. Two: I make you Chief Scribe and Keeper of the History of Incunabula." She handed him a fat notebook, its pages empty, and a pen of solid gold. "Record faithfully what you see. If it hadn't been for you, we would not have known what plagued this land or how to solve it. But you knew, and you brought us Marietta. For that we owe you much thanks." She leaned forward and kissed him, and to everyone's great surprise, he didn't fall down on the spot.

The grand procession was over, and the real celebrations could begin. There were lots of presents for Marietta from grateful Incunabulans: cheese from the Emperor of Cheese, who brought only his finest wares for Marietta to sample; an elegant grown-up gown made from rainbow beads (non-magical beads, this time, but still beautiful) from the Rainbow Maker; a statue of herself in battle with the Dark Prince, made entirely of chestnuts and polished till it shone from the Chestnut Trolls; a ray of moonlight, trapped in a stone and set in a ring from the Moon-Shadow Tigers ("if you need us, turn the ring round on your finger three times, and we will come, no matter where you are," said the he-seeming tiger, "for you are our friend indeed"); from the wizard, an empty notebook, smaller than the one he'd received from the Queen, but glowing with inset stones, for her to record her adventures; and from the Shadowlark, nothing.

"You know I'd give you the last purple berry in Incunabula," he said, looking ashamed at coming to her, empty-winged, "but there are lots of purple berries, and I've nothing else to give."

"Oh, Shadowlark," Marietta whispered fiercely, hugging the bird tight, "there's no gift you can give me that's better than your friendship, don't you know that?"

The Moon-Shadow Tigers were waiting to take her home. The scientists, who had emerged, blinking, from their libraries and laboratories to take part in the celebrations, had decreed that it was safe for Marietta to return home; the link she would ride through, on the back of a Moon Shadow Tiger, opened on Earth just to the left of the mirror in her bedroom.

And so Marietta said her good-byes. There were no tears, no sorrow or regret, no heavy sadness to weigh her down, for she knew she would be back, as many times as she wanted, whenever she pleased. She would have many adventures with Shadowlark on her shoulder, and she reminded herself to wear a purple shirt next time she came. The stains would not be so noticeable then. She hugged the lamp-keeper and Nellie, she hugged the wizard (who managed to keep his feet) and the Storyteller, she hugged Shadowlark and promised him she'd be back soon.

"Hurry back," whispered the Shadowlark into her hair, "who knows when I'll need saving next?"

So many kisses were thrown as Marietta departed, that the flowers finally outgrew the garden and continued up and down and around Quiet Mountain, and the perfume filled the air so thickly that the stands had to be floated further up so that everyone could breathe. There were so many flowers, in fact, that the Queen nearly missed the one she had been waiting for and which now grew, small and lovely, amidst a riot of color and blossom.

Through the darkest parts of the Bleaklands, the Moon-Shadow Tigers ran faster than lightening across the sky, faster than wind through the fields. They knew they must run fast to carry Marietta away, away from the webs that would tangle her, away from the giants who would wear her in their hair, away from the ships that would take her across forgetful seas to the darkest of dark places, so distant and black that even tigers who ride moonbeams cannot go there. Fleet-footed and sure, they brought Marietta home.

"Come back to us when you can," they whiskered, tickling, into her ear. "Close your eyes and let your imagination carry you to Incunabula. Or twist your ring three times on your finger, and we will come for you."

And they ran up the moonbeam that rested on her windowsill and were gone. Marietta looked at the calendar on her desk: the day was the same. She looked at the clock on her wall: no time had passed. Marietta's heart leapt with joy. Her parents had never known she was gone, had never worried or grieved. She could spend all the time she wanted in Incunabula, and not a minute would pass here on Earth.

"What a gift," Marietta said to Mr. Scrumpf, "two lives in one." And with that happy thought secure in her mind, she hugged her bear to her and slept.

Chapter Fifteen

Everyone was terribly curious about this odd habit of flying sideways just one day a week. Most attributed it to the fact that the albatross was cross-eyed, forgetting that he was cross-eyed all days of the week, not just on Sundays. Some were angry and threw sticks, for how dare he fly sideways when proper birds flew right-ways-round every day. Scientists studied him and wrote things down in white notebooks and listened to the air displacement caused by his wings on Tuesdays as opposed to Sundays, and bleached and ironed their white coats every Saturday to be ready for Sunday when the albatross would fly sideways and the press would be watching.

"What have you discovered?" the people asked the scientists.

The scientists cleared their throats and stared at the sky and scribbled in their white notebooks and got inkstains on the fronts of their white coats.

"Not time yet for full disclosure," said one, and the others quickly agreed.

"Certainly not, not by half," the other scientists said.

One Sunday (and it must have been a Sunday, for his flight was definitely east-west and not north-south), Marietta cried up to the bird as he flew by, "Why do you fly sideways?"

"Oh, I get a much wider view of the world this way!" shouted the albatross. "There's ever so many more ways to go than just forwards and backwards, you know."

And Marietta understood.

THE END

Liberty Studio, Inc., Seattle, WA

About the Author

Shannon Perry, born Asolgoth, Queen of the Couch, isn't actually from Earth. She's from Quinthar, 3rd galaxy of the Nimboid Cloud, slightly to the left of the brightest star you can see if you go outside on a clear December night in an even-numbered year and look south and a little west. She won't eat anything with spots, she writes with her nose, and she keeps an ostrich in her living room. She's eleven feet tall and purple. Really.

Author Biography by *Perfectly Frank*

Correction: Shannon Perry was actually born on Earth, in Lawrence, Kansas, though she grew up in Central Illinois. She lived for awhile in England, then several years in the Czech Republic where she thoroughly baffled the natives with her terrible Czech. She now spends most of her time hanging out in Seattle with her cat, Clio, and she teaches English as a Second Language at a variety of places and to a range of people. Her greatest achievement so far was in being born Lawrence's first baby of the New Year, 1968. She's 5'8" tall and the purple is wearing off.

About the Illustrator

Anne Dalrymple is an illustrator living in Seattle, Washington with her super fabulous husband, one very intelligent Siamese cat and 3 hives of golden honey bees .

Anne paints in the old-fashioned way with oil paints on treated board. She also illustrates digitally on the computer in a variety of programs such as Photoshop®, Illustrator® and Flash®. Anne was trained at the Seattle Academy of Fine Art and through individual study with established painters. (Despite the best efforts of her teachers and mentors, Anne still loves to use every color she owns and will take on any assignment that lets her paint shiny metal, jewels or bees.)

The cover painting of *Marietta* was done on 1/4" masonite primed with several coats of gesso. She uses either Old Holland® or Daniel Smith® oil paints, and a huge number and variety of brushes. (In fact, she knows she is done painting for the day when she actually runs out of brushes.) Interiors for the book were done in oils on small canvas panels and rendered in grayscale in Photoshop®.

The painting was photgraphed by Richard Nicol and scanned by ProLab in Seattle.

To see the illustrations for *Marietta* in process, go to www.noopnoop.com/mariettapainting.

The Awful Truth about Max
By Shannon Perry
Chapter One

"Max of Earth," read the clerk of the court, "you are hereby accused of being the Dark Prince of Dullardry, of spreading your Creeping Nasties disease around all of Incunabula, and turning the lovely things into nasty things. For example," he said sternly, peering through his glasses over the top of the document he was reading, "you are accused of turning soft, fluffy blankets into horrid, scratchy, itchy blankets that give you a rash and turning bubble bath into dye that turns your body bright green from neck to toe and lasts for months. You-"

"Is all that really in there?" asked the Judge, leaning over his desk to see the document.

"No," the clerk admitted. "I added that last bit myself." He straightened his tie with slightly green fingers, cleared his throat, and continued: "You are accused of plotting to take over Incunabula and make it a very unpleasant place to live instead of the very nice land of magic it is now. How do you plead?"

"Guilty, I guess," answered Max, looking very small as he stood alone in the dock. "Sort of. But it wasn't just me. I didn't really do it; it was like I was someone else, the whole time." He stopped and scuffed the toes of his shoes over the floor

The High Court Judge of Incunabula (there's only one, so he's awfully proud of himself) leaned forward over the giant wooden desk. He normally sat quietly behind it to show he was concentrating, or rested his feet on it to show he was bored, but when he wanted to be stern and a bit frightening, he leaned over it, and he was doing this now. He *was* rather frightening, really; his big red Judge hat leaned forward with him, threatening to engulf the huge desk and maybe Max with it. Max swallowed hard, trying to ignore the hat and the harsh stare of the Law-and-Order Cat that sat next to the Judge and whispered in his ear.

"Are you trying to tell me," the Judge began, and leaned forward a bit more so he was nearly lying on top of the desk, "that none of it, beginning to end, was your fault?"

(and much later in the book . . .)

Deep down at the bottom of the Pit, for the Pit *has* a bottom, though it's so very far down that not a single boy has reached it yet, something lurked. Something lurked and skulked and crept and slithered, something that had been trapped in the Pit, hurled into the Pit to fall and fall and finally to land. Something chuckled quietly in the absolute darkness. Something hatched plans like evil birds from rotten eggs. Something remembered and was angry; something remembered and swore revenge. Something plotted and mumbled and lurched through dark days.

Deep at the bottom of the Pit, so close to the center of the planet that the ground was warm under the something's feet, down in the complete darkness where even light's long arms could never reach, no matter how much it stretched or stood on tippy-toe, where the darkness was so thick, it had weight, like a wet, woolen blanket, where all noise was muffled and dull underneath the thick, rhythmic thump that was the planet's heartbeat, something wrote a name on the wall, though it was so dark that normal eyes could never see it, had there been any normal eyes down there, and there weren't.

Something wrote a name on the wall: *Max* it wrote, and underlined it twice. Something crept into a corner, a darkness even deeper than the blackest black that can only be found at the bottom of the Pit, for it *has* a bottom, though it's so far down as to make no difference, something crept into a corner. And . . . . waited.

Due to be released in 2003, *The Awful Truth about Max* tells the story of how one good little boy becomes the rotten, horrible, bad-smelling Prince of Dullardry. All kinds of trouble await Max in Incunabula: everyone wants a piece of the Prince who nearly destroyed this magical land, and Max has a lot of explaining to do . . .

The Charles E. Walters Company
330 East 38th Street, Suite 26-Q
New York, New York 10016

The Charles E. Walters Company is a small publishing company with a
large purpose: to provide a venue for gifted writers who are beginning
their public careers. We pride ourselves on being receptive to new authors.
Using the internet and electronic marketing, the company uses modern
technology as an equalizer, giving new authors a considerable platform.
We welcome new manuscripts.

If you want to order a copy of *Marietta and the Creeping Nasties*, or if you want us to tell you when *The Awful Truth about Max* is available, send us this coupon.

☐ Please send me a copy of *Marietta*! $7.00

☐ Please let me know when *Max* is ready!

Plus Shipping & Handling $2.00 (per book)

Total: $_____

Please send a check or money order
for this amount to:

The Charles E. Walters Co.
330 East 38th Street, Suite 26-Q
New York, NY 10016

_____
(your name)

_____
(your address)

_____
(city)   (state)   (zip)

Please allow 2 - 4 weeks for delivery! The Fulfillment Elves of Incunabula are notoriously slow.

Learn more about Marietta or write to the author at www.mariettaandthecreepingnasties.com